About the Author

Belinda Hollyer grew up in New Zealand,
has lived and worked in Australia, and
now divides her time between London and
Key West, Florida. She has been a teacher,
a school librarian and a children's publisher,
and is now a full-time writer. *The Truth
About Josie Green* is Belinda's first novel.
She is currently working on a second
novel for Orchard.

To Ann-Janine,
the best editor in the known world

ORCHARD BOOKS
338 Euston Road, London NW1 3BH
Orchard Books Australia
Hachette Children's Books
Level 17/207 Kent Street, Sydney, 2000, NSW, Australia

ISBN 1 84362 885 6

First published in Great Britain in 2006
A paperback original

Text © Belinda Hollyer 2006

The right of Belinda Hollyer to be identified as
the author of this work has been asserted by her in
accordance with the Copyright, Designs and Patents Act, 1988.

A CIP catalogue record for this book is available from the British Library.

3 5 7 9 10 8 6 4

www.wattspublishing.co.uk

The Truth About Josie Green

Belinda Hollyer

ORCHARD BOOKS

1

When Aunt Aggie gave me the book I thought she was joking.

Well, not at first. At first, when I saw the cover with the all-over dazzle of stripes and spots, I thought she'd brought some cool new thing back from New York for me, because she'd just been there. Which was why she was round at our place having a drink with Mum and telling her all about it. She was perched on the edge of the kitchen table wearing a pair of high-heeled sandals with a model of the Empire State Building set into the heels, like those souvenir snowball things. She was waving a foot back and forth to show how the tiny building floated up and down inside the heel, and waving her glass of wine around as well, while she and Mum were talking.

Aggie isn't exactly my real aunt, but she's the nearest thing to it. She and my mum, they've been friends since they were babies together at the same child-minder. Mum tells a story about how they crawled off after the same toy, and both of them grabbed it at the same time. But instead of crying or fighting about it, Mum says, they just chuckled at each other, and then played with it together. They were best friends all through school, and through their first boyfriends and jobs and everything. So she's not truly my aunt but I started to call her that last year, because, well, because I'd like to have one. We don't have any other close family. Mum was an only child and her parents are dead, and *they* were only children too, so there are no cousins or aunts and uncles for us, on her side. Dad's got two brothers, but like Dad they live up in Nottingham and we almost never see them or their families.

And Aggie is really, really nice, and lots of fun. More like a friend than an aunt, though how would I know what an aunt's supposed to be like because she's the only one I've got. Also, to be completely and brutally honest, when I appointed her as my aunt she seemed to feel more…responsible for me or something, and she does tend to give me more presents than she did before. I didn't think of that at the time, and I couldn't have known it would happen, but I'm not going to pretend I don't like it.

Before, I always thought she gave my sister Fran more presents than me. But I expect it just seemed that way, because of how I feel about Fran.

Anyway, back to the book.

When she saw me Aggie hopped down from the table and rummaged in her bag, which was lying on the floor where she'd dumped it. (Which is *so* Aggie, Mum doesn't let us leave our stuff lying around but Aggie does it all the time, and Mum just raises one eyebrow and never tells her off.) Anyway, Aggie found the book and tossed it to me as she parked herself back up on the table, and I thought – well, first of all I thought it was some sort of handbag. It was soft and shiny, like one of those curvy little bags you tuck under your arm. Which I don't know that I would use exactly, but I sort of saw myself with it, showing it off at school, just for a second as it flew through the air. When I caught it, though, I realised it wasn't a bag at all.

It was a book, with a squashy cover, and you can buckle it shut.

But with blank pages! Like a school exercise book, which I admit was a disappointing first thought.

Aggie was watching me over the rim of her glass, and she could see my surprise. She grinned at me.

'You're always making up stories and games, Josie,' she said. 'I thought you might want to write them all down in one place. Or keep a diary,' she added. 'Your mum and I kept diaries when we were at school. We hid them under our mattresses in case *our* mums discovered our secrets, and read out the good bits to each other in the middle of the night when we stayed over.'

I took a closer look. The paper was lovely, all smooth and shiny, and it smelled nice too. I've always noticed the way books smell. Aggie's brother Don brought me back a picture book from Canada when I was little, and even then I noticed straight away that it smelled different from my other books. Mum says the printer's ink must be different in Canada. Or maybe the paper. Whatever: I don't know why, I have to say. But you have a sniff, and see for yourself.

So anyway, I'm going to give Aggie's idea a try, although I'm not sure exactly what to write in it. I might keep a diary, like she and Mum did – although I suspect my life's not usually interesting enough.

I might do an ideas notebook. My teacher Ms Macintosh says writers keep them, and if you put down ideas when you think of them, they can inspire you later on. I might possibly want to be a writer because, like Aggie said, I do make up lots of stories but I don't always write them down. So that's something I could do with it.

Whatever I decide I'm going to keep it private. It could be somewhere to say things that really matter to me.

The Truth About Josie Green And Her World, Without The Boring Bits.

For example, the truth about me and Fran.

Mum and Aggie always say they're like sisters, but they're not. Sisters aren't as good together as they are. And I should know. Because Fran is my sister, but she doesn't feel like one at all – not how I know they should be.

Sisters should LIKE each other, like Mum and Aggie do. They're always getting together and giggling and going out to movies and the pub. They talk to each other all the time – on the phone or texting silly jokes if they can't see each other, and mostly they meet every day unless Aggie's away. Mum once said they tell each other things they haven't told another living soul.

'Like what?' I asked, wondering what sort of things were ever that secret. Mum laughed, and said, 'But Josie, if I told you—'

'They wouldn't be secret any more,' I finished for her. But Mum said that the things she and Aggie told each other weren't necessarily top-secret. 'Just stuff no one else would care about, a lot of the time,' she said. 'Like – oh, like how I hate the hair on my toes and that's why I don't shave my legs because you can't shave your toes, it's too hard to do them properly. Aggie shaved them for me once, but they still went all prickly and horrible, so now I use wax or hair remover instead.'

Gross! Too much information! I wrinkled my nose in disgust, but Mum didn't take any notice.

'And, oh, a million things: how we *truly* feel about life,' she ended vaguely.

So, I still don't know. To be brutally honest, if all they talk about when they're together without me and Fran is the hair on their toes, then I'd be sorry for them. But I know they share things – everything from mascara to margarine, Aggie once said – and support each other in times of trouble, and look out for each other as a matter of course. One time Mum decided she had to lose some weight, and if you saw Aggie you'd know how ridiculous what she said to Mum was, because she's as thin as a rake, but the moment Mum said she had to start watching her weight Aggie said, 'I'll do it with you.' Automatically. Just to help Mum.

They're very different people but somehow that's OK, they don't seem to care that Mum's mostly serious and calm, while Aggie's more inclined to be over the top and intense. Their differences just kind of slot together.

But with me and Fran, the real sisters in the family, it's a joke.

One and a half years and a world of difference apart, Mum says, but it's more than that. To be brutally and completely honest, I don't like Fran. Not half as much as I like some of the girls at school. Bryony, for instance, she's the closest to a best friend that I've got right now, and she's – well, she's actually *nice* to me for a start, which if you have Fran in your family isn't what you expect. Bryony listens to me, even if she doesn't agree with what I say. But with Fran, everything starts with a sneer. She ignores me most of the time and when she doesn't do that she's rude.

Me and Fran, we don't even *look* like sisters. I have dead straight hair and freckles, I'm not very tall for my age, my big toes are smaller than the rest of my toes, and I love reading.

Fran is tall and thin and bony with lots of frizzy hair, and all she ever does is sports. We don't have a single thing in common.

She's not my true sister, she just can't be.

Can you divorce a sister?

2

I was fiddling with my new book in bed last night, wondering what to write in it, and Fran came in and didn't say anything at all. I *know* she must have been interested, I would have been if it was me. She even pretended not to notice I was still awake which annoyed me, and of course that's exactly what she wanted. Then she put out the main light without even asking, which really got to me. I had to reach out and switch on the spotlight next to my bed, which I don't use if I can help it because it's too bright and makes my face hot. I didn't say anything, but I seethed with crossness for ages, and couldn't get to sleep. I lay listening to Fran breathing in the bunk above me. (Snoring, actually.) I knew there was no point in complaining because she'd pretend to ignore me. Then I'd *really* lose it.

I wish I didn't have to share a room with Fran. Sometimes the wishing makes me feel slightly sick, because I want it a lot. But there isn't anything else for it, because, like Mum says, we don't have another bedroom, just hers and ours. And Mum gave us the big one when we first moved into the flat, after Dad left. I actually think it was nice of her, because she *could* have chosen the big one – she earns the money to pay the mortgage so she should have first choice.

But I don't think Mum really understands just how much I don't like Fran, and it's hard to tell her because she doesn't like me saying so. She lectures me about my attitude and bangs on about how Fran's going through a difficult stage, and how I have to try harder to get along with other people.

Well, I do. I try a lot. Even Ms Macintosh at school says my social skills improved last term, which to be brutally honest just means that I haven't hit Samad again, like I did at the start of the year when he tripped me up on purpose and my lunch went all over the floor, and he smirked. (Not for long though, ha ha.) In fact now I think about it, it's Samad's social skills that have improved, not mine. He hasn't tripped up anyone else since I hit him.

But anyhow, Fran is the giddy limit, like Aggie says about her boss at work.

Maybe I could sleep in the hall? I might measure up for my bunk at the weekend.

That's just me being over the top.
I know I can't really sleep in the hall.
I don't even *want* to sleep in the hall.

Maybe Fran can sleep there, and leave me the bedroom?
Yeah, right.

One good thing, though: I've decided what to write in my new book.
We started a history unit about families at school today, which is what inspired me. I thought it would be deadly when Ms Macintosh announced it, because it's a mixture of history and English with citizenship, and in my experience, combinations like that can be rubbish. Last year some teachers got us doing something called What Rome Taught The World that combined everything you can think of, science and maths and history and English and even P.E. All it meant was that we spent ages outside in the freezing cold measuring footsteps and miles and calculating straight lines, which was a completely boring timewaster.

But I perked up when Ms Macintosh explained what she meant, because it sounds like being a detective. Which I now realise I could be: Josie Green, Family Detective.

We have to research something about our families, like proper historians do. We can go for the recent past, or even further back if we know anything about that, and these days lots of people do know because family history's on the Internet and TV and everywhere. Ms Macintosh showed us slides of old family photos, and paintings from before there were photos, and got us talking about what the people looked like (stiff as boards and miserable, most of them) and what they might have been thinking when the photos and paintings were done. ('Help! My brain has been stolen by aliens!' was what Bryony muttered to me, looking at them.) Then she gave out copies of real documents from history, and we had to say what we could find out from them. My group got a letter from 1666! It was a girl writing to her mother, and at first we couldn't make sense of it. But Ms Macintosh said to read between the lines and deduce the facts from the evidence, and when we tried that, it was amazing what we could work out. Just like detectives!

One thing was, the girl, her name was Mary, wrote that there was 'little good news' to tell her mother, but then she said that someone called Henry Webster had made her a gift of sugar and ginger. So we decided Mary didn't like Henry Webster or she'd have been happy to see him and pleased about the sugar, which turns out to have been wickedly expensive in those days. (If someone brought me a bag of sugar I'd have to wonder about them, so times change.) Also, Bryony said maybe Henry fancied Mary but she didn't fancy him back, and *that's* why the sugar news wasn't good. I even wondered if her parents might *make* her marry Henry for the sugar, so I realise that being a detective could be the thing for me.

Anyway I told Mum about the research project when I got home, and how I wanted to do mine about her and Aggie. She gave me a funny look, one of those 'should I say this to a child?' looks. It frustrates me. I am not a child, I am twelve for pity's sake, which is next door to being a teenager. Although if Fran is an example of being a teenager, I don't look forward to going there.

'Don't you think I can use Aggie?' I argued.

'I do; she's as much a part of our family as anyone. She's my sort of honorary aunt and your better-than-a-sister, and she's always here, and...'

But Mum said she hadn't meant that, and of course I should include Aggie if I wanted to.

'No, Josie, I just wondered if these days, research about families is such a good idea. Lots of people have such muddled lives with stepfathers and half-sisters and brothers all over the place. Won't some of them be embarrassed because they don't have an ordinary family?'

But to be brutally honest, there are so many mixed-up families in my class that what Mum means by ordinary families are the odd ones out. Lots of us have parents who don't live together, and have new fathers or new mothers, and spend their weekends going to visit the other halves of their parents, and aren't around for sports or movies or sleepovers. Bryony's parents broke up last term and it's really hard on her, she hates not having her dad at home.

And then there's people like Samad who's Bengali and has stacks of family here and in Bangladesh, and almost more aunties and uncles and cousins than he can remember. Which is a whole lot more fun than Kirsten's family. Her mother has just got married again to her third husband, so Kirsten now has two little brothers, three if you count the new baby, who have different fathers, as well as her own father who is in Australia and married again with stepchildren. Kirsten can't keep track of who she's related to, and she says she doesn't even want to, all she wants is to stay in one place for long enough to put up her own posters on her own wall above her own bed, and not panic when she wakes up in the night because she can't remember where she is.

My family is sort of in-between. My dad, he's called David Green, used to live with us, but he and Mum split up when I was in nursery school, and we don't see him all that much any more. When he left, Mum and me and Fran moved into this flat and Dad lived with Aggie's brother for a while, but then he moved back north.

Fran and I don't look like him, not that I can see anyway. He's tall with curly black hair and he's called a mechanical engineer, which basically means he travels around looking at pipes in factories. Truly. That's a job.

I used to wish that he'd come back and live with us, or that we'd all go up to Nottingham and live with him, but I don't now. Not really. When I got to proper school and saw other kids going off with their dads I wanted us to be a proper family too, all together. That was before I realised that how you look from the outside doesn't count; it only matters what's on the *inside* – how everyone is with each other. You can only consider being a proper family on the inside, that's where it really matters.

And if only Fran was different, we would be a proper one.

I'm not sure how I feel about Dad. I don't remember him all that clearly from when he lived with us, so to be brutally honest I can't say I miss him from then, can I? I suppose Fran misses him more than I do, because she was older when he left and more used to him being around. One and a half years more used to him, now I think about it. Not that she'd tell me about it.

He used to visit more when he first left, when he was still in Don's spare room. I looked forward to him coming; I liked having a Visiting Dad. He took me and Fran to the park and the zoo and he took us to *Peter Pan* one Christmas which was my first play ever, and he cuddled me when I was frightened of the crocodile and started to cry. (I *was* only six.) When he took us to the play of *The Lion King* he loved it almost as much as I did. He didn't stop raving about the animals that dance up the aisles, and trying out the lion mask from the programme over supper, so he's fun to be with.

He doesn't come so much any more; his job changed and he's off all over Europe looking for pipes to inspect. But he still sees us when he can and he sends postcards from everywhere, separate ones to me and Fran so we don't have to share them. And he phones when he's away, and sometimes we go up to Nottingham for the weekend.

I don't feel all that close to him, though. So when he first arrives I'm a bit shy and then by the time I've got used to him all over again he's gone. He's interested in us, though, which might sound funny – why shouldn't he be, he's our father? But what I mean is, when we talk he really listens to what I say. He's good like that. Better than Mum. Not better than Aggie though, she's super good at listening when she's around.

On the other hand when Dad goes away again it's much easier. He and Mum are always polite to each other when he's visiting but you can feel the tension in the air, and after he goes Mum is different. Like she's been holding her breath.

I don't exactly know what went wrong between them but I don't think it will ever get better. I don't even think about it much, to be brutally honest.

Bryony just wants her parents to get back

together again, that's all she thinks about. But I don't. I just think about Fran.

Anyway. Now I know how I am going to use Aggie's present. I'm going to put my research notes for the project in it, all the stuff I find out about my family, like you do when you are a proper historian. Or better yet, like when you are a famous detective, which I may well be one day. Then, years into the future when I am dead, someone might find the notebook and use it to work out what my life was like. I have to say I hope I don't die tragically young, because I've only just started the notes and they'd be complete rubbish at this stage.

3

This morning I woke up when it was only just getting light. I didn't have to get up for hours, so I wondered why I was awake. Then I realised that Fran was moving around the room. She was trying to be quiet, but even so I felt annoyed. I don't like waking early, I'm not a morning person. Mum says I get that from *her* mum who never even wanted to talk before eleven in the morning. On the other hand, I don't so much mind waking up early if I can lie thinking about things and then drift back to sleep again. But I couldn't go back to sleep once I knew that Fran was up, I was too curious about why. I mean, *why* would anyone be up so early if they didn't need to be?

And then I remembered about the notebook, and my new plan to be a family detective. I could start practising that very minute, on Fran!

Mum's always saying things like *Seize the day*! which means, make the most of your opportunities when you have them. Well, here was an opportunity to start detecting, and I didn't even have to get out of bed to do it! How good was that?

I pretended to stay asleep, and luckily I was already lying on my side so all I had to do was open my eyes a crack to watch Fran in secret. She was getting dressed, and she'd got as far as jeans and a T-shirt, and was breathing hard as she tugged at the laces on her trainers. I almost giggled out loud because Fran always makes a big production out of it. She just yanks her feet out of them at night, and then the next day she has to faff around untying the bow and loosening the laces to get them back on, and since she never has enough patience to do it properly, her feet get stuck halfway.

When she finally left the room I listened hard, to work out where she'd gone. You can tell by the sounds in our flat what people are doing and where they are doing them; you just have to know what to listen for. For instance, there's a loose board in the hall outside Mum's room that makes a clicking noise. It's soft but you can't mistake it. No matter how quiet she tries to be,

I know immediately if Mum comes out of her room at night – if I'm awake, that is.

It can even wake me up. When I was seven and had tonsillitis and Mum was coming in to check on me in the night, I used to wake up the moment she trod on that board. Then I'd lie there feeling miserable with my sore throat but glad she was on her way to me; glad that in a minute she'd be sitting on the end of my bed, gently patting my feet and asking me how I was.

The kitchen door often squeaks, and it's on one of those swingers that makes it click back into place. You can hear the click if you listen for it after the squeak. I listened hard because I thought Fran might be going to make herself breakfast. But the squeak/click didn't come.

Instead, I heard the front door easing back into its frame with a 'thock' sound. You have to pull it firmly to get it to click into place; that's what makes the thock. If you try to close it by twisting the key in the lock it doesn't shut properly. You have to make it make the noise, to be sure that you've locked it. Mum calls it a clunk-click, like an old car seat-belt ad on TV that Aggie's brother Don jokes about. But in fact it's really more of one single sound.

Where on earth could Fran have gone so early?

I thought of following her to find out, but the luxury of being in bed alone in our room, with at least an hour before I had to get up, was too great a temptation. I snuggled down and drifted back to sleep. I didn't even think about what had happened until I was at school. Then, it made me curious all over again.

Where had Fran gone? And why?

When I got up at my usual time she was sitting in the kitchen eating breakfast (and with her bum parked in the chair I like to use, of course). And to be brutally honest it had turned into such an ordinary morning by that time, I didn't get back on the detecting trail until later.

I know it won't be any good asking her straight out so I've started writing this down in my detecting book so I can have the evidence on record.

I just *knew* I shouldn't have asked her! It was an entirely rubbish thing to do and I wish I had kept my mouth shut.

I hate how she is with me, and I hate her. Why is she always, *always*, so mean?

I bet if I had been the one to get up in the middle of the night and creep out of the house, she would have asked *me* where I went. And she probably would have told Mum as well, which as I could point out, I have *not* done.

She was all sneery when I asked her, and she went, 'Oh wouldn't you like to know all my secrets, and wouldn't I *love* to tell you them – *not*! Do you honestly think I would tell a stupid little baby like *you* anything that mattered?'

And then she narrowed her eyes and sort of hissed at me, 'And don't you *dare* tell Mum, little tattle-tale. You'll be sorry if you do.'

Well I wasn't going to anyway, so there.

Mum says Fran knows how to push all my buttons, and I shouldn't let her get to me. If I didn't react Fran would soon stop being mean, Mum says, except that she calls it teasing me, not being mean. Mean is, however, what she is. And anyway, Ms Macintosh says teasing is just a step on the road to bullying, which is *definitely* not OK.

I do not believe Fran would stop tormenting me if I just reacted differently to her. I think she does it because she likes to, and that's that. It's just the sort of person she is.

But what I know for sure is that something strange is going on, and I intend to find out what it is. And then I could turn my notes into a *real* mystery story, instead of a game of detection.

The Mystery of the Disappearing Sister.

Maybe it would make a good thriller?

Anyway, I think I will definitely be a famous detective instead of a famous historian. I expect that detectives make a shed-load more money than historians.

4

Fran did it again this morning. Sneaked out early. If she does it one more time I will definitely follow her.

I've written more notes about My Disappearing Sister, although I can't make her my school project. I still want to do that about Mum and Aggie. I'm going to interview them separately and ask them the same questions, and see if they give the same answers. Like on TV, where they find out how much married couples *really* know about each other. I am willing to bet that Mum and Aggie know more about each other than any other two people on this Earth, so I'll have to put in some trick questions to make it harder.

So anyway, the notes about Fran so far are just the dates and times of when I know she was out. This is evidence, like when police read out their notebooks in court, and I will be able to prove that she did it.

Not that I'm going to have to prove anything, though. I'm not going to tell Mum, not yet anyway. Not because Fran threatened me about telling on her. Because I would hate it if *I* was sneaking out for some reason and Fran told Mum on me. And from now on I am going to try behaving in a mature and responsible way, like how I wish that people would behave towards me. Ms Macintosh calls this Being Mature, although to be brutally honest it sounds to me more like Very Hard Work.

We talked about it in school yesterday – not me and Fran, I mean about being mature. Ms Macintosh asked us to agree some rules about our behaviour, and what we expect of ourselves and each other. This was after Daisy pushed Nikki so hard that Nikki bumped into the library shelves and hurt her elbow, and when Ms Macintosh asked Daisy about it she just said that Nikki had pushed her first.

Ms Macintosh got cross about it. 'For pity's sake,' she said, 'you can be more grown-up than that! You can do *better* than that! You don't have to lash out when someone pushes you, you have a choice, Daisy – all of you. Think about it! Be responsible for your own actions! Be *mature*!'

It could sound like Ms Macintosh is a nag or a drama queen, but she's not. She does bang on a bit which is boring at the time but she's fair, which works in your favour if you are even halfway to reasonable. And our group – well, we had Nikki in ours and she can talk all day about anything and usually does – anyway, *we* thought everyone should try to behave like we wanted people to behave to us no matter what they did to us. So if someone pushed us, say, we shouldn't push back just to repay the bad deed, because we wouldn't want that done to *us*.

'What if it's a war, though?' asked Nikki. 'What if it's a war and someone comes and shoots at you, wouldn't you want to shoot them back and forget about being mature?'

'Not if you're a pacifist,' said Bryony. 'If you're a pacifist you just have to let people get on with shooting you.'

'And it's not a war, dumbo,' Samad pointed out. 'It's just rules for our year, to stop people being mean.' He threw a sour look at Nikki, who is well known for doing a lot of pushing, only this time Daisy had got back at her.

He got a very sour look back from her and she muttered, '*Dumbo?* Thanks, *fatty*,' under her breath. But Samad ignored her, or maybe he decided to be a pacifist, and the moment passed.

So anyway, I started to realise how this could help at home. What I thought was, Mum could be right about me letting Fran push my buttons. Fran annoys me so fast it's unreal; Aggie calls this getting up someone's nose, and Fran gets right up mine. And after that's happened I'm so angry and upset, and so far into '*I hate her! I hate her!*' that I can't think straight.

Maybe – just maybe – if I could find a way to wait and count to ten, like Ms Macintosh suggested, I might not mind as much by the time I reach ten. I might think that whatever meanness Fran put on me was *her* opinion, and *her* problem, and that I didn't have to agree.

And wouldn't she get a surprise if I didn't rise to her bait! If I ignored her. She's never been ignored by me, that I can remember.

I had a chance to try it out this morning. When I got up Fran was back from wherever she had mysteriously been, and having her breakfast like before. I put some bread in the toaster and went to the fridge for juice, but I couldn't see the carton. I was poking about in case it was hiding behind something else when Fran said, 'Looking for something?' I turned around and she was tipping the last of the juice from the carton into her glass, and smiling triumphantly. Then she drained the glass and licked her lips deliberately, looking straight at me. Spoiling for a fight, like Aggie might say.

Well, I like juice for breakfast and to be completely and utterly truthful I *did* mind that Fran had finished it. But I was so keen to try out my plan that I was almost pleased she had been so mean! I looked straight back at her and shrugged my shoulders, like I couldn't care less. Then I took one of Mum's herbal tea bags. I don't much like them but the fruit ones are sort of OK, and I thought I'd have one of those instead of juice.

My toast popped out just how I like it. The water boiled. I put the teabag into my favourite mug, and sat down. Fran just sat there looking at me. I buttered my toast, taking my time getting it right out to the crust before I looked back at her. When I did, I was amazed at how surprised she seemed – well, confused, actually, like I had taken the wind out of her sails. I shrugged again and bit into my toast, then sipped the tea, and kept my face blank. But secretly, my heart sang with triumph and I felt like it was my birthday.

It had worked!

Maybe I can rise above my petty feelings, like Ms Macintosh said we should.

Maybe I can even ignore Fran.

Well, maybe later on I can ignore her, but not right now – not while she's doing this disappearing act. I am going to stay on her case and find out where she is going and why. It will be good detecting practice to look for clues and deduce the facts.

5

Something just happened and I'm going to put it in my book, which is filling up faster than I expected. I don't know exactly what the new happening means, but I can tell it means *something*...

When I got back after school Mum wasn't home but Aggie was, sprawled all over the kitchen table working on her laptop and muttering to herself about sales targets, so I didn't interrupt her. You have to get your timing right with Aggie. When she's there for you she's in your face as large as life but when she's not, you might as well shout into a bucket for all the notice she takes. I sort of admire that in her, although to be brutally honest it is frustrating at times, but Mum says that's why Aggie's done so well at her work, being so single-minded.

I think it's funny that Mum gets Aggie to be at the flat after school, when Mum can't be there herself, but Aggie probably wouldn't notice if we were there or not. We could be someone else's children. Or ram-raiders. Or alien invaders.

Anyway, then Bryony arrived because we were going to Samad's house together, because his cat has just had kittens. Bryony thought her mother might let her have one to cheer her up about her father leaving, and she wanted to choose it now, in case that happened.

I just wanted to look at them. I like cats, but we haven't had a pet since Mum's cat Dinah got run over two years ago. Mum was so upset, well I was too, but Mum was really cut up. She said it wasn't fair to have an animal when we were all out all day and that was why, she said, Dinah had got run over because she was bored and lonely waiting around for us all day and had wandered off to find entertainment. And Dad gave Dinah to Mum when they were still married, so probably it was sad because of that, too. Because of the Dad thing being over, or because she'd had Dinah for so long, I can't tell. Maybe it was both.

When Dinah died Mum said we could get a gerbil or a hamster if we liked, but Fran said she was too old for them, and I don't much like little pets in cages. I like them bigger, and I also prefer the way cats cuddle up to you and you can have a conversation with them. Dinah was Mum's cat but she liked playing with me too, and sometimes she slept on my bed. When I had tonsillitis she used to spend all day with me, which was a great comfort. No way can I imagine being comforted by a gerbil.

Anyway Samad's cat's kittens are lovely, five teeny tiny ones all different, two girls and three boys, and Bryony picked the one with spots all over his teeny tiny tummy. *So* cute. We couldn't play with them or even stroke them because they are too new, they haven't even got their eyes open yet, and Mimi the mother cat wouldn't like it. She has to protect her babies when they're small and weak, and if strangers touch them then the kittens might smell wrong and she could get upset, maybe even abandon them. Still, it was nice to see them.

When I got back home Mum and Aggie were both in. I came into the hall without them hearing me close the front door because they were playing a CD in her bedroom and talking. *Yuck! Hairy toe talk!* I thought as I stood in the hall, taking off my jacket and hanging it up, and wriggling out of my trainers so I could walk around in my socks, which is what I like to do.

Just then, though, the CD went into a soft swoopy bit and I heard their voices. Mum had been talking when I came in, I'd heard her voice without listening to the words if you know what I mean, but it was Aggie's words I heard now.

'She doesn't look like him, does she?'

And then Mum.

'Oh, kids take a while to grow into themselves. Have you noticed how Josie looks just like David when she smiles, now? Maybe that's how it'll be with her.'

Aggie again.

'I hope she doesn't end up *being* like him!'

Mum again.

'Oh, don't say that, Aggie. He's changed. We all have.'

I froze in horror.

Us! They were talking about us!

Actually, if I'm truthful, my first thought was, they were talking about *me*. I only got to the Fran bit later.

They must have heard that I was in the hall, even though I didn't move or say anything, mostly because I was rooted to the spot with curiosity. Anyway, suddenly there was a meaningful silence in the bedroom, and then Aggie leaned around the door and saw me, and then of course they stopped talking about me (and Fran) and started talking about other stuff. I made out I hadn't heard anything anyway, and the moment passed.

I thought about it later, though, when I was in bed.

What did Mum and Aggie mean?

I hadn't known about looking like Dad when I smiled, but it felt OK. I've probably inherited his smile, like with Mum's mum's early morning habits. That's what happens in families.

But what about Fran?

They *must* have meant Fran, mustn't they, with the other stuff they said?

What had Aggie said, exactly?

That – who? Fran? – didn't *look* like him. And how Aggie hoped that she (Fran?) wouldn't end up *being* like him.

But what was all that about?

Why was it OK if I was like Dad, and not for Fran?

And did Aggie mean she didn't *like* Dad?

That couldn't be it; Aggie was fine about him. Sometimes they were a bit sharp with each other when Dad came down and Aggie was around, I'd noticed that, but mostly they're OK. Aggie thinks Mum is better off without him, I'm sure, she says

Mum's happier now she doesn't live with him. I bet even Mum thinks so.

Oh! Oh! A thought suddenly hit me, like a flash of light. I almost sat up in bed; good thing I didn't though, I'd have hit my head on the bottom of Fran's bunk. So I just lay there in the dark and listened to Fran's slow breathing, and thought about the amazing idea I had just had.

What if Fran had a different father!

It kind of made sense.

If Aggie and Mum had actually been talking about Fran—

And *if* they had been talking about a father that she didn't look like—

It could mean Fran's father wasn't the same as mine.

Couldn't it?

Wow.

Oh, double wow!

Maybe this has something to do with Fran disappearing?

Say, if she's discovered who her father is, she might be going out to try to find him!

The Family Detective swings into action!

I'll write up my notes in the morning.

6

I don't know who said that pride comes before a fall, but whoever it was is unfortunately right. My mature behaviour with Fran has bitten the dust already, although to be honest I am surprised it lasted at all. I had the pride bit for most of yesterday, and I enjoyed every nanosecond of it until this morning, when it fell flat on its face.

The trick is, acting in a mature way needs lots of attention all the time. It's like being some sort of mental fitness freak, hopping around keeping your mature behaviour warm and ready to use. I found that out today. I had only stopped hopping around for a few minutes and I'd only *just* taken my eyes off it and bam! I was back into the old bad ways with Fran.

What happened was this. I expected her to get up early again and go out on her Mysterious Journey, but she didn't. So I was already less than happy with her, because I'd got all prepared to follow her. I had pushed my jeans and sweater and trainers under my bunk, so I could pull them out and put them on as soon as she left the room. I'd even left my knickers and socks on in bed, under my pyjamas, to be super-ready. I'd imagined finding clues and writing up my notes, and everything.

I do not like to make plans and have them not happen. *And* I woke particularly early, which of course I also do not like to do.

No Fran moving about. I listened carefully. She was still in bed; I could hear her breathing.

I thought maybe she'd get up in a minute. I made myself stay awake so I could be prepared, but she didn't. So by the time I had to get up anyway I was tired and cross. *And* my left sock had come off in the night which I only realised after I had finished making my bed, so I had to unmake it again and reach down the back for the sock, and I bumped my head really hard when I got back up.

So when Fran sneered at me when I didn't want toast for breakfast because the bread was stale, and made a 'poor little baby' routine out of it, I just lost it, to be completely honest. I admit that.

I burst into tears, I threw the rest of the loaf at her (and missed, what a shame) and only when Mum came in to see what was wrong did Fran stop chanting at me in that infuriating way of hers.

'Josie-wosie, sucks her thumb.'

I used to, when I was little. It's not a crime.

Mum made me go into the bedroom while she talked to Fran, and then she brought me back into the kitchen and we had to say we were sorry to each other. But Fran had to say it first, I noticed, and when I only mumbled it in a way that Mum would usually say was ungenerous, she didn't make me say it again in a nicer way. It also looked like Fran had been crying, which surprised me. Maybe Mum was in one of her strict moods – she certainly looked serious. That should have comforted me, to have her a little bit on my side about it, because she doesn't usually take sides. But I still felt unhappy.

Because it was Saturday I didn't have school but I did have my recorder lesson. Mum makes us learn a musical instrument, no argument, and the only choice we have in the matter, she says, is which one. I picked the recorder because we play it at school in the orchestra, and the music teacher gives us lessons at a special price, and it's easy to carry around. Once I'd got past 'Three Blind Mice' I even started to like the sounds it makes.

Fran chose the piano just to be difficult I expect, because we don't have one. She has to stay at school to practise it, which serves her right.

Anyway, I had to get to Mrs Watts's house for my lesson, which means being at the bus stop by ten past ten, or I don't make it in time. So I was hurrying to get ready when Aggie put her head around the door and offered me a lift in her car. I hadn't even heard her come into the flat, but I was really pleased to have a lift from her. For one thing we wouldn't leave for another fifteen minutes, and for another thing it meant I'd get to ride in her extremely cute little car. Mum has a car, but it's an old banger and it often won't start on cold or rainy mornings – or as Mum points out, in any month with an 'r' in it, and sometimes on just about any day with a 'y' at the end. And it doesn't look great. Mum doesn't care what her car looks like and just says, well, it gets her there, but *I* say it might not get you back again. And in all honesty I DO care what it looks like. I have been known to be embarrassed to be seen in it.

So Aunt Aggie and I drove off in style with her car engine making *vroom-vroom!* noises, and the sunroof open, and a great CD playing. I just wanted to sit and enjoy being out with her, like we were best friends, like her and Mum. But right away she wanted to talk about what had happened with Fran that morning, which slightly spoiled the effect.

'Your mother phoned me, you know,' Aggie said, 'after you and Fran had your fight at breakfast.' She rounded the corner of our road with such verve she almost took a traffic bollard along. ('Verve' is a new word I have acquired, and this is the first chance I've had to use it, since two days ago when I had to read out loud in class. Ms Macintosh said I did it with expression and verve, which turned out to be a good thing.) The bollard made her slow down, and she glanced at me to double-check I had my seat belt fastened, but she didn't stop talking for a nanosecond. She was definitely the full-on, no-holds-barred Aggie this morning.

'You don't think I'm interfering, Josie, do you? Nosy-parkering? Sticky beaking, like they say in Australia? Say if this makes you uncomfortable, you know you can say *anything* to me.'

I shook my head; I didn't have to say anything out loud because she kept glancing at me. I didn't mind that she wanted to talk about it; Auntie Aggie is family, like I said before, so I kind of expect her to come out with stuff. But I wasn't going to be blamed about Fran, and just feeling that Aggie *might* blame me made me nervous.

'The thing is, Emma is really upset,' she went on, frowning at the traffic now that we were coming up to the busy shopping centre. (Emma is my Mum's name.)

'Me too,' I muttered defensively, staring out of the window. Maybe someone from school would see me, which would be nice because of the car and because Aggie was looking so terrific. She never wears worn-out sad old clothes like the rest of us, *all* her clothes are for best, she always wears make-up, and she generally has some new, up-to-the-nanosecond way of doing her hair as well. This morning she practically looked like a model, except that she's not tall enough, not that you can see she isn't when she's sitting down driving. But worse luck, I couldn't spot anyone I knew in the Saturday crowds.

Aunt Aggie glanced at me again with both eyebrows pulled up into a question mark. Mum does one eyebrow; Aggie does both at once. It looks seriously cool when they do it and I have tried raising just one like Mum or tenting them together like Aggie, but the effort makes my face twist which isn't the effect I am looking for.

'I-DID-NOT-START-IT,' I said, staring straight ahead and spacing the words out slowly and loudly. 'Fran was mean to me. She *always* is mean to me. Sometimes I don't mind much, but other times I do. This morning she upset me, and so I cried and threw stuff. I couldn't help it, Aunt Aggie, it all happened before I could think.'

My voice went a bit husky because I suddenly felt worse about it. Mum being worried enough to phone Aggie – well, it didn't bother me *that* much because she phones Aggie all the time anyway. But Mum had probably asked Aggie to talk to me, or anyway she knew about it, which made it more serious, like getting a warning from the Year Head instead of just your own class teacher. But still, I only wanted to get even with Fran for making me feel hurt and stupid and cross.

'Aunt Aggie, Fran just doesn't like me. She picks on me *all the time*. It's like bullying,' I added, remembering what Ms Macintosh had said, and I suddenly felt that was true. Fran *did* sort of bully me. The way I felt when she had a go at me at breakfast was how you feel if someone is tormenting you at school. You feel small and defeated and there's no one around to be on your side. It happened to me in primary school, so I know.

Aggie suddenly signalled left, and pulled into

a parking spot. She switched off the engine, undid her seat belt, and turned to face me.

'Josie, the trouble is that Fran is jealous of you,' she said.

I blinked with surprise.

'Why would she be?' I asked. I couldn't imagine even one reason for that. Fran's much better known at school than I am because of her sports thing, people respect her for that. And what Bryony says is that Fran's tall, so people can easily point her out to each other when she wins a race, or whatever. I'm too short to be pointed out, even if I did anything to make me a celebrity, which so far I haven't.

'Because – oh, because Fran was an only child until you came along,' said Aggie slowly, sitting back and pushing her hair back away from her face to tuck it behind her ears. 'She was used to having things to herself when she was little,' she continued. She fiddled with the indicator instead of looking me in the eye, which was a bit of a relief at the time, although I thought about it later in a different way.

'It was OK for a while, though. You two were fine a few years ago, weren't you?' Aggie added.

I didn't answer; I was trying to absorb what she was saying, and wondering about what I'd overheard, too. Did any of this fit with Fran having a different father?

But Aggie wasn't waiting for a reply, she just swept on.

'And now you're both older it upsets her again, having the competition. It's not that she doesn't love you...' Aggie put her hand on my shoulder to stop the disagreement she could see rising up on my face – 'you are her sister, after all. But it's hard for her, and—'

But if we might have different fathers, were we really sisters?

I felt a bit panicky, like it was all a bit much to take in.

'So it's my fault? Is that what you're saying?'

Aggie leaned over and gave me a quick hug. Her sweater was soft and silky, and brushing against it felt like stroking feathers.

'No, my darling Josie, of *course* not. You mustn't think that.'

'So it's *Fran's* fault?' I still felt sulky. 'If it's not my fault it must be hers, right? She's to blame?'

Aggie patted my shoulder and sighed.

'Josie my love, my dear little honorary niece, it's not that simple. Blaming *Fran* isn't going to make things better, any more than blaming *you* would. Let's try to move on from this recrimination and unhappiness, to a calmer and better place.'

I wasn't too sure what recrimination was, but Aggie often says weird things, like she's just come from one of those huggy-feely courses where grown-ups bang on about their emotions and relationships. Movie stars and celebrities are always doing that sort of thing. Talking about moving on to a calmer and better place would embarrass me if it was anyone else, but Aggie's just like that. She talks about star signs and auras, too.

'What we need here, is for everyone to take responsibility for their actions,' added Aggie, beating out a rhythm to accompany her words on the steering wheel. *For* – bam, *their* – bam, *actions* – bam.

'So *Fran* has to take responsibility for being mean to me?' I asked. I wanted to get that bit clear.

Aggie nodded. 'And *you* have to take responsibility for what *you* do, too, when she upsets you. As *she* has to, if you upset her.'

'But how is that going to change anything? Why will Fran stop picking on me to begin with?' In fact I sort of saw what Aggie meant, but I didn't want to give in too easily.

Aggie smoothed back her hair again, and ruffled

mine, as far as mine can be ruffled. Then she started the car, and signalled to pull out into the traffic.

'Trust me,' she said. 'I *can* get you to your music lesson on time, and I *know* this will work. Your mother and I *both* know it will work as long as everyone pulls together. And Emma's talking to Fran right now, getting her to agree as well.'

I still had my doubts. Why would Fran be changed by anything Mum was going to say to her? Mum had said lots to her before and as far as I could tell, it hadn't done any good. I did wonder if I should mention Fran's mystery trips, but since I'd decided not to tell Mum I couldn't tell Aggie either: it'd be the same thing in the end. Also, I wasn't sure about the maybe-different father. I wanted to think about the clues some more, and decide what else I needed to know.

But I felt better after Aunt Aggie had talked to me. I thought that, deep down, she understood what really went on. She hadn't said so out loud, but when she's on line and attending, Aunt Aggie makes me think that she really understands. Understands *me*, Josie Green.

Dad can do that too, like I said, but he's not here much to do it. Mum can do it if she really tries, but mostly she's too busy to hear what I'm trying to say. I can tell she's really thinking about something else at the same time, which is not encouraging.

I do wonder why Aunt Aggie said Fran was jealous of me, though. First of all, I find that hard to believe. I can do some things Fran can't, but they aren't things she cares about. I would know if she minded about me reading lots of books, for example. But she doesn't. She doesn't like reading unless it's about sports.

And second of all, there was something funny about Aggie when she said it. I can't exactly explain, but she suddenly stopped looking me in the eye. The way she talked about it wasn't exactly right.

Like *she* didn't believe it.

So why say it?

I have written down what she said in the notebook. Now I need evidence about where Fran goes, and I'll be close to solving that mystery. Which will only leave the Dad mystery to solve, and the whole thing's done!

I must say, prepping for the Mum and Aggie interviews isn't as interesting as this.

7

I followed Fran this morning, and I know more about *what* she's doing. But I still don't know *why*.

Being a detective is actually harder than I had expected, even with the notebook. The clues I was looking for? They're only the start, I've discovered. When it's real life and you spread the evidence out in front of your nose, it doesn't just turn itself into a story. The clues could actually make a whole lot of different stories, depending on how you put them together.

I didn't wake up when Fran got out of bed, but I did when the front door went *thock*.

At first I just lay there because I didn't exactly want to get out of bed, I was too warm and comfortable. On the other hand I was curious. Extremely curious, to be brutally honest, as I got more awake.

Like, aching with curiosity.

And I'd promised myself I'd follow her next time.

So I got up and pulled on my clothes, grabbed my socks and trainers, and tiptoed into the hall. You don't have to pass Mum's bedroom door to get to the front door of our flat, but you do have to move quietly so as not to disturb her – she's quite a light sleeper, and she's also an early riser like Fran. (Not *this* early, though.) But there was no sound from Mum's room, and I got out the front door and closed it as quietly as I could. I stood on the landing for a minute, putting on my socks and trainers and listening hard in case Mum called out, if she'd heard the door close. Nothing! So far so terrific, as Aunt Aggie would say.

But I didn't know what to do next. Fran had now been gone for about five minutes, which meant I couldn't follow her because – *doh!* – I didn't know where she'd gone.

Our flat is on the ground floor of the house; there's another one upstairs and a basement flat under us. I didn't think Fran would have gone upstairs. We don't know the couple there well, just enough to say hello to when we met. I know Mum's talked to them about the roof and fixing the entry system on the front door, but that's all. Fran and I don't even know their first names; we just call them Mr and Mrs Carson. I didn't think

Fran could have secretly developed a close relationship with them and gone up to watch their cable TV, which we do not have.

The basement flat was more possible, because the woman who lives there is friendly with us. We call her Rose because she asked us to and not because we have forgotten our manners, like Mum first thought. But I was fairly sure that Rose was still away. She works for a museum and she'd gone to Turkey to look at some ruins; she knows all about the way people lived in ancient times. In fact she'd promised to give a talk to my class about family life back then, for our project. That's why I thought she wasn't back, because first of all she only went last week, and second of all she'd have said she was, and come up to see us.

Anyway, third of all, Rose is more my friend than Fran's.

And fourth of all, what would Rose's flat have to do with Fran looking for a father?

But I know that detectives follow clues even if they seem unpromising, so I went out the main front door and peered down at Rose's door. I couldn't see any lights on inside. It looked like Rose *was* still away—

Oh, how double dumb of me! We had a spare set of Rose's keys, just in case there was some problem

55

like a burst pipe and we needed to get into her flat to put it right. She'd given them to Mum ages ago. Why hadn't I checked to see if the keys were still in the kitchen drawer?

I glanced up and down the road. There was a bit of traffic, and people waiting at the bus stop on the corner. But there was no sign of Fran, and no clues about where she might be. (Later I thought, well, what would be a clue? Someone holding a sign that said: *Fran went that way?*)

I crept back through our front door. Still no sounds from Mum's room, and still about fifteen minutes to go before her alarm clock went off. I hung up my jacket without rustling it and tiptoed along the hall.

'Josie?' The sleepy voice came from Mum's room. *Blast, double blast, and knickers. And hairy toes.*

'Mum?' I answered, but kept walking. Maybe I could check the key drawer before I went into her room—

'Josie!' Louder this time, less sleepy. Mum hates it when we try to have a conversation with her from another room. She always says, if she calls us she doesn't mean: *Let's shout at each other through the wall so neither of us can hear the other one properly.* She means: *Please come in here now, so we can talk in a civilised fashion...*

'In a minute!' I called quickly, to stall her. I hurried into the kitchen, and opened the drawer where Mum keeps spare keys.

And Rose's keys weren't there.

I admit that I felt slightly triumphant. I had solved the mystery of where Fran was going in the mornings. But only slightly, because I still didn't know why, or what she could be doing alone in Rose's flat.

Also, I had to deal with Mum's questions. *Had I just come into the flat? And where had I been? Didn't I know that I couldn't just come and go without telling her? What was she supposed to think if she got up and found me missing?*

I had a hard time answering the questions. I just muttered something about checking the post, which sounded daft because our postie almost never gets to us before I leave for school in the mornings. But Mum didn't seem to remember that.

It was harder not to tell Mum about Fran disappearing, specially now I knew where she was going. Mum would be furious about her going into Rose's flat without permission. But it never occurred to Mum that Fran was out too. She knew we never did stuff together if we could help it, so the idea that we could have done the same thing at the same time wasn't a natural one to have. And Fran came back into the flat while Mum was in the shower (*How did she manage that?* I thought resentfully) so Mum didn't hear her, and she *still* didn't realise.

I don't know how to tackle Fran again, if I'm going to. I'd rather not if she's going to be horrible about it, but to be honest I'm a bit worried now. What if she's doing something in Rose's flat that she shouldn't? Not just going there, but what if she was going through Rose's things, or taking things, or—

I started to wonder if I was wrong about my father theory. Maybe Fran was meeting someone in the flat – like a boy? We'd just had a social worker come to school and tell us about chat rooms on the Internet and about not giving anyone our real names or addresses, or meeting them in the real world. So I wondered if Fran could have done that, got caught up in some weird and dangerous thing. But, well, we don't even have a computer at home; only Mum's laptop when she brings it from work, or Aggie's sometimes. But they aren't keen on letting us use their computers, not even for school stuff. They always hover over you saying things like 'Don't download that without checking it for viruses!' when you weren't going to download anything anyway. We use computers and the

Internet at school, but no way can you get through to a chat room on those machines even if you want to. So I couldn't see how Fran could set anything up however hard she tried.

A boy from school seems more likely.

Fran's two years ahead of me at school so we don't have anything to do with each other there, even if we wanted to, which – surprise! – we don't. But I've sometimes seen her with boys; not lovey-doveying around with them though; just walking along with the ones who are mad keen on sport like she is. I think they were probably just going in the same direction to gym or the practice fields, to be brutally honest. I never heard she was interested in any of them in a personal way, and at our school, someone would most likely tell me. It's not a good place for privacy.

And I decided my other ideas couldn't easily be true either. Fran was mean to me, and difficult even when she wasn't being mean, and something was going on with her that wasn't right. But she isn't a thief; she wouldn't be taking stuff from Rose. What's more, she *is* my sister, or at least I think she is. So I ought to look out for her, even if she's older than me and even if she's a complete pain.

If she's in any kind of trouble, I want to help.

8

So now what?

A whole lot of questions and not enough answers, is what.

Starting with overhearing Mum and Aggie, although I'm still trying to work out what they meant. And if they *did* mean that Fran doesn't have the same father as me, what then? Like, if it isn't Dad, then who could it possibly be?

And now there's also what in the world Fran was doing in Rose's flat? And, how am I going to find out?

I don't know much for certain, not yet, I just have suspicions. I'm still writing it all down in my notebook, though, which is halfway to the answers.

I had to talk to Fran about Rose's flat, but I didn't know how. And what happened was, I just did it!

Fran was in our room doing her hair. It's very

thick and curly, and so after she washes it she lets it get just about dry, and then she brushes and brushes it. It floats around her head and it looks amazing. Not like human hair, like something from another planet, almost. When I was little, Mum used to do it for her and I loved to watch, and I used to say that Fran had fairy hair.

In fact, if I'm honest, there have been times when I wished I had hair like hers. A few years ago I wanted to have a perm to make it curl all over like Fran's but Mum said no, and after a while I stopped wanting that anyway. (I have been growing mine for weeks and now I can just about scrape it into bunches which is encouraging even if they do make my head sore. Soon I can have plaits like Bryony's. Or maybe just one fat plait down my back, like Samad's sister Leila, who can sit on hers. Not that you'd want to sit on a plait for long unless you wanted to prove something or win a bet, because Leila says it's very uncomfortable.)

Fran didn't immediately frown or snap or say something mean when I went in, so I sat down on my bunk and grinned at her. She looked surprised but she did grin back, and then she asked me to pass the hair slides from her top bunk. Maybe she's trying to be a bit nicer? Anyway I thought it was as good a time as any, and I jumped right in. (Jumping right in is the same as seizing the day, according to Ms Macintosh.)

'I know where you're going, early in the morning,' I said. I tried to sound ordinary, like I was talking about the weather.

Fran put down her brush and turned around, but I knew I couldn't let her say anything; we'd just end up shouting at each other, and my plan to solve the mystery would be as good as dead.

So I just held up my hand and said, 'Don't start, Fran. Let me say this.' I must have had surprise on my side, because she took a breath but didn't let it out in mean words. She just looked at me.

'I know,' I went on, 'because I was curious and I followed you. I didn't see where you went but then I thought of Rose's flat and the keys weren't in the drawer. So then I was sure.'

'So?'

Fran didn't deny it. Then I really *was* sure! I decided I might make a good detective after all!

'So, I want to know why. I bet Mum doesn't know what you're doing, and I won't tell her unless I have to. But Fran, what are you doing, going into Rose's flat?'

Fran was still just staring at me. Sometimes she does that, she just stares straight-faced. It can put you off, but this time I just stared right back.

I wasn't going to let her get away with that if I could help it.

Then something happened to change how I felt. I saw that she had started crying! Her face didn't move or crinkle up the way it usually does when people cry, she was just still staring at me, but she had tears running down her face.

I was completely stunned.

I went over and put my arm around her without really thinking why, just wanting suddenly to comfort her. She didn't pull away; she didn't respond at all. And the tears still trickled down her cheeks.

So I gave her a bit of a hug. I suddenly felt like her older sister, and I said, 'Tell me. Tell me what's wrong.'

'I just wanted something to myself,' she said in a wobbly voice, but I didn't know what she meant.

'Rose's flat? Rose's flat is something to *yourself?*'

'Oh, I don't expect you to understand,' Fran said, with a flash of anger. 'Why should you?' She'd stopped crying but she looked like she might start again any moment. Her cheeks were still wet and the tears had dripped down the front of her T-shirt.

'Try me,' I said. 'Tell me what you mean.'

Fran took a deep shaky breath, wiped her hand across her face and tossed her hair back.

'I want something – somewhere – that's mine. Private. Where I can be by myself.'

I stared at her. She looked at me and smiled. Not a friendly one though; a mean sort of smile.

'I don't expect you to understand. Why should you?' she repeated.

'I might do,' I said slowly, 'but I still don't see what you mean about Rose's flat.'

Fran picked up her hairbrush again but didn't use it; she just sat picking at the bristles. Then she turned back to me.

'If Rose isn't there I can be by myself, with no one else around, just for a while. Which is a whole lot better than nothing.'

'But – what do you *do* there?' I was genuinely curious.

'I don't *do* anything. Or touch anything much. Sometimes I read for a while. Today I just made a cup of tea and listened to the radio.'

'By yourself.'

'All by myself.' Fran's voice sounded different when she said that, but then she went back to sarcastic again.

'For about fifteen minutes, Josie, that's all. *And* I washed up the teapot and the cup afterwards, *and* I tuned the radio back to the boring station it was on, so you needn't think I'm making a mess. Rose won't know anyone has been there.'

'Fran…'

She stared at me again. Less blank than before but still a sort of mask, keeping me out. I tried again.

'Do you – is it because we have to share a room?'

'Sort of.'

'But I *do* understand that. I don't like it either. Not much anyway,' I added hastily because otherwise it sounded rude and I didn't want to upset her more than she was already. But I don't think she even heard what I had said.

'I'm older than you,' she said, and she suddenly pulled away from me and sounded passionate instead of blank. 'And I have to share with you when I don't *want* to, I want some space that's only *mine!*' She was almost shouting by the end of that, and she sounded pretty desperate. Desperate and miserable.

'But – what will you do when Rose gets back?' I asked her. *This is seriously weird*, I was thinking as I spoke. *I've gone from thinking that Fran was doing something she shouldn't, to worrying if she will be OK when she can't do it any more.*

'What do you think I'll do? I'll stop, of course.

I've done it before.' Fran picked up her brush and started pulling it through her hair again, like the conversation was finished.

She'd done it before? Like, how many times? Rose was often away. Had Fran done this for years? Or just recently?

But I just sat there on the floor beside her, and didn't ask any more questions. Fran finished brushing her hair and fastened her hair clips, all in silence. She turned to go, but then she stopped and glanced at me.

'Thanks, Josie.'

And then she went out of the room.

Thanks for what? I wondered. For listening? For trying to understand? For not telling Mum? Fran hadn't thanked me for anything for ages, so I was sort of touched that she'd said it, whatever the reason.

I've put everything down. And I've added two more things.

I think what Aggie said to Mum is right; Fran isn't anything like Dad. (I don't know who she *is* like, though.)

I wonder if she could be adopted?

9

So then I did a lot of thinking.

I thought about how Aggie was right; Fran and I *had* been OK when I was little. She'd been my big sister and she'd looked after me, and I'd looked up to her. I remembered it all when I was thinking about her hair and how I'd called it fairy hair.

Her hair is still an amazing sight. But we aren't friends now, and I don't know her any more. I don't even know if she's really my sister.

I thought about sharing a room, too. Maybe I could have realised that Fran didn't like it any more than I did. That didn't change the fact that we had to share, but maybe Fran *did* need more space and privacy now she was older. Maybe that was even why she'd got so mean.

But most of all I thought about Fran getting up when it was dark and sneaking down to Rose's empty flat because she was desperate for some space to herself; for some peace and quiet away from sharing a room with *me*. That hurt a bit, but I could hardly complain, because I wanted it as well.

Then I remembered Aggie saying Fran was jealous of me and I wondered if that was true, too? Maybe Aggie had sounded odd because she was exaggerating to get my attention the way grown-ups sometimes did – the way Aggie did, anyway. If it *was* true it made me feel uncomfortable. I won't say Mum doesn't treat us differently, but when she does it's only because we are two different people. That's what she says. She treats us equally but differently, she says.

Nikki at school says she *knows* her mother likes her little brother more than her, she's always playing with him and Nikki says her mother never played with *her* when she was little. (I don't see how she can remember that for sure, but it's how she feels.) But the thing is, I don't think Mum likes either of us more than the other one, I honestly don't. Part of me wishes that she did, of course, if it was *me* she liked more than Fran. She, Mum, she's strict with us both, stricter than lots of other mums. But my point is, she's strict with both of us, she doesn't play favourites. (Once she said that she had to be strict because there was only her; Dad wasn't around to help out with discipline, and he just did treats when he came to visit. She sounded cross about that and I can see it doesn't seem fair to Mum, but that doesn't stop me enjoying Dad's treats.)

So if Fran does feel jealous it can't be that she thinks Mum loves me more than her. I know that isn't true, and Fran must know it too. So I had to come back to the dad theory. I asked myself, if Dad wasn't *my* real father and I knew it, would *I* be jealous of Fran? And the answer is, probably I would be. So that could be another clue, not the sort you can exactly prove, but the sort that feels true in your heart.

Could I maybe make things better for Fran as well as me? Could she have a place to herself, without having to go down to Rose's flat and hide? I know I said about one of us moving into the hall, but that was just a joke. No one could live in the hall with everyone coming and going and pushing past their bed. But maybe we could improve our room?

It's quite big, like I said before. Our bunk beds stack against one wall, then there's the window wall, and opposite that are the wardrobe and the dressing table which we share. The door wall has shelves for books and a pull-down table where you can work. I like doing homework at the kitchen table because I enjoy noise and bustle while I work, with the radio on and Mum and Aggie coming in and out. Fran does hers in the bedroom with the door closed because she likes silence, and she wants to concentrate without getting distracted.

Could we move things around? Divide the room into two, even just hang a curtain down the middle? I didn't know about the wardrobe and the dressing table – maybe they could be in the middle. The big problem would be the bunk beds, because they're stuck together and you can't shift one of them by itself.

And then I thought of asking Aggie! Her non-stop positive attitude means that if something's a problem, you can rely on Aggie to say: *it's not a problem, it's a puzzle to be solved!* And maybe her brother Don would help. Don's very good at DIY, he's always doing stuff at his place; big projects like moving whole walls and putting in new bathrooms. With any luck, our bunk beds would be a pushover for him.

It might all cost too much but I've decided not to worry about that, I'll ask Aggie first. If she thinks there's a way, I bet she'll talk Mum into it. Or maybe Dad would pay, if I asked him.

My detective stuff is coming along. I just looked back at what I've written so far, starting with the first date and time when Fran went out (to Rose's flat, I now know). Then what I overheard Mum and Aggie say. Then my theory that Fran has a different father, which could fit with Aggie saying she's jealous.

I was wrong about Fran going off to look for him, though, because – *doh!* – she wasn't looking for him in Rose's flat. So I need more clues about that. I'll think about who it could be, if it isn't Dad.

I don't suppose Fran's actually adopted. People only adopt if they can't have babies themselves, don't they? And Mum and Dad could: they had me later on.

I haven't done much on my research project lately. I've only written down the title I thought of: 'Better Than Sisters: The Story of Emma and Aggie'. I have to think up questions to ask Mum and Aggie. I could even start on Aggie tomorrow, if I see her about the room.

10

Aunt Aggie *loves* my idea about the bedroom!

I didn't tell her about Fran going to Rose's flat, because I still think she'd tell Mum even if I asked her not to. So all I said was Fran was unhappy sharing a room and so was I, and couldn't we maybe split the room to make it more like two separate ones, or at least so there was proper space for each of us?

Aunt Aggie nodded, frowning and tapping her teeth with a fingernail. I'd borrowed Bryony's mobile at school and asked her to meet me afterwards, and Aggie said she'd take time off work if it was important, and I said it was. Well, it is. I must say I appreciated that, and Bryony was impressed when I told her. Adults often ignore things being important to *you*. As Bryony would be the first to say, because there's still no sign of her parents getting back together, no matter how much she tells them that's what she wants.

Aggie and I met in the shopping centre, but first she whisked me off to look at some new boots – she couldn't decide which she liked best and she needed my advice, which was cool. I loved the ones with really high heels and wrap-around ties, with tassels on them. *Completely wickedly wonderful*, I told her, and so she bought them.

Then she took me to the new café that's all metal and glass – well she would, it's her sort of place. The wait staff, which is what Aggie says is the modern thing to call waiters and waitresses, however silly it sounds, wear total black and carry these hand-held computers and tap into them with your order.

Aggie had tiny coloured spots painted on her fingernails, which look so funky. I was worried the spots would come off on her teeth while she was doing the thoughtful tapping but they didn't. I also thought of doing mine that way, maybe Bryony and I could do each other's, although since we aren't allowed nail polish at school we'd only have to take it all off again.

Anyway, like I say, Aggie agreed with me right off and the tooth-tapping was just her thinking how to make it work. She said that the fact I'd had the idea showed that I was a creative thinker and able to think outside the box. I don't know about a box but

I like being known for creative thoughts, it sort of goes with verve. And it also goes with being the Family Detective, which I will get back to in just a minute because I have a new Possible Clue.

'I haven't mentioned it to Mum yet, because of money. It might cost too much,' I added as I slurped my smoothie, but Aggie dismissed that idea as I'd hoped. Her job pays a lot of money and she always has some to spend on us as well as herself – more than Mum does. Mum teases Aggie and says all her money goes on her back, which isn't strictly true because Aggie spends lots on us. She's a bit like a fairy godmother as well as an honorary aunt, for instance when we go to a movie it's Aggie who pays for everyone. Unless Dad's there in which case he does.

'Josie, my dear niece,' Aunt Aggie said in a lofty manner, waving her arm around and almost clipping our waitperson on the nose, 'money will not be a problem, I promise you. I will help, and your dad would help if I asked him, and Don can do a lot of it. He can do the heavy lifting – the grunt work.'

I had to laugh about the grunt work but I didn't want Aunt Aggie asking Dad for money, it felt awkward for some reason. But Aggie said she'd talk to Mum and I wasn't to worry, and Mum would check with Fran to make sure she was OK with it. She must have seen I was worried about Dad being asked for extra money, because then she said maybe we wouldn't bother Dad. 'It probably won't cost much,' she said. 'I bet we can manage.'

No surprise, Fran was pleased when Mum asked her. And Mum was for it too, of course, thinking that it would help smooth out our troubles.

Fran didn't go to Rose's flat again before Rose got back, which was last night. Well if she did I didn't wake up, so she must have been super quiet. She hasn't snapped at me, or been mean since we talked. But on the other hand she hasn't actually said *anything* much, which makes me think that the problems are not yet behind me.

And now the thing that could be a New Clue. Don was here with Aggie last night to look at what needs to be done to the room. I sort of like Don, but not as much as Fran does. She's crazy about him. She always hangs around in the room when he's here and listens to him when he talks, whatever it's about and however boring it gets.

Don's OK, though he can be a serious bore when he's droning on about cars and football. That's what he does for a living; not football, and not droning on, either. Cars. He fixes their engines.

It's almost as bad as Dad's pipes. Dad and Don talk engines whenever they're together, you have to separate them if you want a more interesting topic.

Fran loves it all. She talks sports with Don, they go on about who has just won the hundred metres or shot their put or done their dash, it's not just football. But it's also football, because Fran plays soccer, as anyone in our whole road must know since she's always banging on at top volume about *that*.

Anyway, back to our room. The bunk beds turn out to be the sort you can unscrew from each other and then stand up by themselves. So we can have one on each side of the room, which Don said he could do, no problem.

'And we could maybe put up a panel in the middle, to here—' said Mum, waving her hand to show where a divider might go.

'A screen would be better,' said Fran. 'One of those folding ones. We could decorate it, one side for each of us.' She glanced at me, and I nodded agreement.

'Good idea!' called Aggie from the hall, where she was paying the pizza delivery boy – we were having takeout for dinner, her and Don included. She popped her head around the door. 'I know where to get a folding screen, I'll go this Saturday – want to come, you two?'

She meant me and Fran. Fran and I don't do stuff together if we can help it, but I could tell Aggie was trying to get us doing something together that wasn't squabbling or fighting. And I thought I should help Aggie, as well as help choose the screen. Fran's mind must have been running through the same thoughts, because she nodded, and so did I. Aggie looked smug.

But here's the thing. The Possible Clue.

When Don was fiddling with the bunks, Fran went across to help him – to hold the screwdriver. She bent over and he was kneeling, and so their heads were on a level.

Their hair is just the same!

Don's hair is short and Fran's is long, and it's a different colour because Don's is pale red and Fran's is light brown. But – and I have never noticed this before, so I must be developing some full-on detecting skills now – it's the exact same *kind* of hair. All frizzy and bushy and stand-out-y.

I don't see that Don could be Fran's father, I really don't. I mean, Mum doesn't even particularly like him – she doesn't *not* like him, but she doesn't, for example, pointedly ignore him the way you do when you were keen on someone and now they're an embarrassment. She just doesn't seem to rate him. At least I don't *think* she does.

But it makes me wonder.

In the end we didn't do all that much. It wasn't like a TV makeover, although I was looking forward to gasping with astonishment when I saw the result, like they do just before they burst into tears and say how they hate it and it's complete rubbish and how much they hate purple AND the best friends who chose it.

Our room isn't that different. We haven't even painted the walls again, because they didn't need it. I had an idea that we might do our sides of the room different colours, but we've left it for now. We could still do it later.

So. Don moved the beds and we've put up the screen. I'm going to do a collage with the postcards that Dad's sent me, and even if Fran covers her side with stupid football posters I won't care because I won't ever have to see them.

We got new reading lights and tables beside our beds. Aggie and I put the tables together AND Fran said thank you for doing hers! To be honest I'm good at stuff like that, which surprises even me. I was going to be sarcastic to her about how it isn't just the Fans of Don who can do stuff, but (a) first of all I remembered in time that I was trying to be nice, and (b) second of all I only thought of a good pun I could have teased her with, about the *Frans* of Don, ha ha, much later on.

We've moved our books and posters, mine are all on my new side and Fran's are all on hers, and the same thing with the dressing table – my drawers are the ones on my side of the room. We can't divide inside the wardrobe but that doesn't matter much. The only thing we can't change is the table, it's on Fran's side of the room, but since she likes using it for homework and I prefer the kitchen, that doesn't bother me.

When she looked at the finished product Mum said, why on earth didn't we do something like this when we first moved in? In fact she behaved a bit like the people on makeover programmes, oh-ing and ah-ing and carrying on. But I don't think we needed to do all this when we moved in, because me and Fran weren't enemies. I am writing this sitting up in my bed propped on the squashy pillow that Aggie bought, one for each of us, and using my new bedside light. I can keep my notebook down the side of my bed, I've made a secret pocket for it against the wall and no one will ever know where it is. Which is excellent as hiding places go, and a whole lot better than under the mattress, which I now realise is a rubbish place.

When we were moving stuff I found an old photo album which had got lost behind a box of toys. I haven't seen it in ages, and maybe I can use some of the photos to go with the 'Better Than Sisters' tape I am planning. I even found one of me and Fran when we were little, standing with Aggie and Don, and their mum and dad who are dead now, but I remember them. Aggie's mum used to make special cakes for us with our names in icing, when we went to see them.

Anyway, I was right – Fran's hair looked like Don's even back then. His hair was longer in the photo and you can see it clearly.

Why have I never noticed that before?

11

I admit that things have improved. Fran is never going to be my best friend and I am never going to be hers. It's never going to be like Mum and Aunt Aggie. But it's definitely better than before. She *did* snap at me this morning when I cleared her plate off the table and she hadn't finished breakfast, but that's the only thing so far. And believe me, I am keeping count.

To be brutally honest though, there's a disappointed bit of me that imagined we'd become friends and share secrets from either side of our screen, or something dorky like that. I couldn't share my secrets with Fran anyway, so, like Bryony says, I should just get over myself.

Bryony says I should be grateful for *definitely better*. She says that if Fran is mean to me less often, and if I also have a better bedroom, then what's the problem? Bryony is really very practical and is turning out to be good at making the best of bad situations, which I admire in her. She's noticed that her mum and dad are actually nicer to each other since they got separated, so she's going to try to stop banging on about them all getting together again, and see if that helps even more. It might, and anyway it will help everyone who's friends with Bryony. I don't like to be mean, but we are *very* familiar with her problem.

It's hard for her to give up on her parents getting back together, because it has been her dream since her father left home. And although she hasn't said she's *actually* given it up, she is on the road to that. (She is also on the road to having the kitten! Her mother says she can, she's so relieved that Bryony's less gloomy. I have pointed out that a kitten is probably not all she could have; her mother might even agree to a pony right now. You have to get your timing right.)

I haven't shown Bryony my notebook or told her about my detecting, though. I don't think I should. Some things have to stay private.

Last night in bed I remembered what Mum and Aunt Aggie said, and I thought again how weird it was. If I didn't know better I would think I invented it. If I hadn't written it down right away, I might even think I had.

But I didn't invent *what I heard*. I have just put together clues and now I am trying to reach a conclusion. It isn't just detectives that do that; historians do it all the time, according to Ms Macintosh. They piece together a story based on the available evidence. Well, that's what I'm doing.

The conversation came back into my head because the family research project at school is gearing up. (That's what Don says when stuff is moving along fast, he says it's 'gearing up' like in a car engine; I'm going to try that out on Dad next time I see him, I bet he will appreciate it.) We're making a wall display called All One Human Family, about us all. It's interesting to find out about other people's families, I can tell you. Daisy is doing a tape like me, but hers is of her family having dinner, which is very funny and includes her father saying 'elbows off the table' *seventeen times*. And I thought Mum was a nag! Nikki's got an old journal from her great-great-grandfather who lived in China. Kirsten's done a map showing where she goes to different parts of her family, with pictures of them all waving and saying 'hello!' and 'goodbye!' to her. Samad says he will have to bring his *nani*, that's his grandmother, to school so she can explain his family because it's too complicated for him. He's trying to do a diagram but it stretches for ever, it would cover the whole room if he put it up.

When Rose came up last night she brought some real Turkish Delight with big chunks of nuts in it, practically whole nuts, and it is completely delicious. She had a glass of wine with Mum, and I had more than my share of the Turkish Delight because Fran was out at soccer practice. But I would point out that I did leave some for her.

Rose has fixed a day with Ms Macintosh for her talk. She's going to explain how people often lived in big groups, like tribes, and not in small units like we have today. She said that children didn't necessarily stay with their mothers and fathers, they might not even know who their birth mothers or fathers were, and whatever adults were around looked after whatever children needed to be cared for.

I thought that sounded a bit like us with Aggie, because she looks after us when Mum isn't there, but when I said that Mum got all snippy with me and said it wasn't like that *at all*, and then she changed the subject. I don't know why she jumped on me. I have noticed grown-ups do that when they think outsiders shouldn't be told something, but Rose knows that Aggie's Mum's best friend and spends lots of time with us, it's hardly a secret. Also

I think I was right that Aggie's part of our family group, and Mum shouldn't mind me saying it.

Mum was still cross with me later. What I thought was, I could use a photo of Mum and Dad and Aunt Aggie and Fran and me for the display. When we started the project I didn't plan to include Fran, so it shows how much things have changed. Or maybe how much I have changed. Or probably that Fran has changed. Anyway, I thought I'd find one of Fran and me as babies, with the three grown-ups. Or if there wasn't one photo of us all together I could do a collage.

Anyway Mum said no, there weren't any photos of everyone together when me and Fran were little. She was all definite and dismissive, like *that's the end of this conversation*. I was sure she was wrong so I checked the photo boxes on the hall shelves, and even the old album in our room. But she was right.

There's Fran and Mum. There's Fran and Aggie and Mum and even one or two of just Fran and Aggie. There's me with Mum. And me with Mum and Fran. (I was only just crawling in one of the photos, and I have to say I look SO cute I might use it for my project.)

And there are stacks of Fran and me with Dad over the years. Whenever he takes us somewhere he gets other people to take pictures of us with his camera and then sends us prints. I used to get embarrassed when he asked strangers but that was silly, no one minds doing it, although sometimes the people you ask are rubbish at it and you get the pictures back all blurred. Or with no feet. Or even with just feet. You have to pick the right strangers.

But I couldn't find everyone together. It doesn't matter much, I can copy bits of people from the photos I have, or photocopy all the pictures and then glue parts of them together. But I think it's strange.

Maybe it shows I was right about what I heard.

Maybe Fran and I *really* don't have the same father, like I suspect.

I wonder if Mum could have been with someone else, the mystery man, *before* she was with Dad?

Maybe there are pictures of him – Fran's mystery father – and Mum has hidden them!

The other thing was how Mum acted when I asked her for the photos. She sort of was like, *that's not something I should have been asking about.* Or maybe more, *that's something I wish you wouldn't ask about.*

She was already cross with me, but I don't think that was all. It was more like she had something to hide. And OK, we don't have the photos, she was right, but it was as if it was *on purpose* that there aren't any pictures.

I have been trying to work out what to do with the clues. I have written down the possibilities in my notebook, and here they are.

<u>Number One</u>.
First of all, I could ask Mum straight out.
I don't want to do that, I have to say. It's sort of a weird thing to do, and Mum isn't going to tell me if it is true, at least I don't think so. Even just thinking about asking her, I feel embarrassed. The thing about Mum is, she isn't that easy to talk to, and if she doesn't want to discuss something it's hard to make her understand that OK, *she* might not want to talk about it, but I *do*.

That was always how it was with me and Fran, until just recently. Fran would be mean to me and I would go to Mum about it and she would not want to hear. She wasn't exactly mean to me as well, but she would dismiss it like it wasn't important or it didn't matter, or like I was exaggerating. She'd raise one eyebrow and say something like, *I don't think Fran meant to hurt you, Josie darling.* And then she'd ignore anything that proved Fran *had* definitely meant to hurt me, like the time Fran tore my favourite poster *on purpose*. Mum ran her finger over the tear and said Fran might not have realised she had torn it, but the corner was hanging right off! It's sometimes like Mum lives in another universe. So trying to ask her, *does Fran have a different father from me?* I don't think I'd get an answer I could trust.

Number Two.
Second of all, I wondered if I could talk to Aunt Aggie about it.

The plus side is that she would be easy to talk to about it, and if she was in a mood to listen to anyone, she'd listen to me. She really tries to understand me and she would absolutely get why I wanted to know, but the question was, would she tell me? On balance I have decided that she probably wouldn't, because if Mum hasn't told me and doesn't want me to know, then Aggie would have to support her, on their best-friends-better-than-sisters agreement.

Number Three.
Third of all, there's Dad.

I tried to think of a way to ask him next time I see him. One problem is getting time with him alone, which I almost never do. I'd have to make a big deal about setting that up, and that could make it even more awkward than it was already. If we were just together by ourselves, maybe I could casually bring it up in conversation. *Oh by the way Dad, are you, um, Fran's father?* I don't exactly think so! And what I'm not allowing for is if Dad *isn't* her father, but he doesn't know he's not! Or, say he *does* know but he doesn't like to talk about it.

Another problem is that if Dad knew that Mum hadn't said anything to me then he might not either. They're not together but they do get their stories straight with us most of the time. For example, Dad doesn't let us do stuff that Mum won't. This was a big disappointment to me the first time I tried, when Dad first came back after he'd left and took us out. We went to a film and I asked if we could have a giant tub of popcorn each and Dad said no and then – just like Mum would – he reminded me that we had both been sick all over the seats the last time we'd had too much popcorn. He even *sounded* like Mum. It was creepy.

Number Four.
So fourth of all, I could try to find out another way.

I can't think of one right now but it must exist: I just need to find it, but it is very frustrating meantime. This is my life. And my family. And

I don't know what's true about it any more. It's all very well doing a project about myself, but if I don't know what the truth is how can I tell it?

I wonder if Fran knows? I can't ask her, though.

I've decided to try what Aggie calls the scattergun approach; which involves a bit of everything.

<u>Number Five.</u>
I'm going to check all the photo boxes and the old albums again. I'll look out for any man I don't recognise *and* I'll count how many times Don is in a photo with Mum, because he may be a long shot but he does exist, *and* the clue about him is rather a good one.

Also, I'll watch Mum without her knowing that's what I'm doing, especially when Don is around or if his name is mentioned. I'll watch them all closely, Mum and Aggie and Don, and Dad next time he's here, and see how they behave, and try to deduce some more clues.

And I'll watch Fran to see if she provides any clues of her own.

To be brutally honest, it's starting to feel like I am spying.

But if it is about me or my family, I think I have a right.

12

Dad arrives tonight! He's been in Amsterdam checking out Dutch factory pipes, and Aggie's going to pick him up from the airport, and what I want to know is, *why*? No one usually picks Dad up. He stays with one of his work friends, or else in a B. & B. near the shopping centre, and then he just turns up at our place.

I asked if I could go with Aggie but then it turned out I had to go into school for the orchestra try-out. (I think I did OK but you never know, and they won't say until next week. The trouble is, there are a lot of recorders to choose from. It's a pity, because I'd like to tell Dad that I am in the orchestra, if I make it.)

Fran wanted to go to the airport too, I heard her asking, but Mum said no. Actually it was Mum who was first going to collect him but she can't, because her car didn't pass its test to stay on the road; it has to have new brakes. (Aggie told Mum that she'd asked Don if he could do the job, but he'd said he wasn't good enough. Heavens to Betsy, as Aggie said, if Don's not good enough, the garage repairmen must be superhuman. Mum just laughed. She didn't sound...anything special...when Don's name was mentioned. So now I'm back to thinking I'm probably wrong about that.)

I wondered if Mum and Aggie wanted to talk to Dad about me and Fran, before he got here. About our fights, or our less fights than before, or our new room, or all of that. I could tell him myself that we've improved. Fran even asked me about my family research project the other night, which is more than she has ever done in her whole life before. I think she wondered about my notebook, and why I keep scribbling in it, but luckily when she asked me I was only writing out questions for Mum and Aggie to answer, so I didn't have to hide the real detective things from her.

I must say, being a detective takes more time than I had foreseen when I started. Not that I mind, because to be honest it's like having a secret. Well, it IS a secret of course. And what I realise is, my notebook is like a bomb. If anyone found it and read it, everything would blow up.

Not that anyone CAN find it. But it's a thought.
I started it for fun, and now it's gone serious.

Mum has been a bit edgy this last week, I have
noticed, since that night with Rose. Mostly edgy
with me, but then I notice it more when it's me.
Like, when I interviewed Aggie on tape last night,
Mum was hovering in and out of the room. I had to
make her go away, because what's the use of trying
to see if they give the same answers to questions, if
Mum's already heard what Aggie says?

Maybe she's edgy about The Great Mystery!
Whatever it is. I must say, I haven't spotted any
more clues. But this weekend, with Dad around,
I might see or hear something new.

Fathers. It *couldn't* be Don, could it? But Mum
doesn't fancy him! Not enough to have his
baby. Yuck.

I started looking through the photo boxes this
morning when Fran wasn't around, not that it would
have mattered because I was only looking on the
shelves in the hall, but I haven't found pictures of
a Mystery Man. It did occur to me that *if* Fran
knows Dad isn't her father, and *if* she knows who it
really is, then she might have a photo of the MM
tucked away. I don't want to search her private

things though, because first of all I'd hate it if she did that to me, and second of all she might catch me doing it. (That second reason is more of a Bryony one, being mature and realistic at the same time.)

I haven't looked through *all* the photos yet, but that is still my aim.

And tonight I will observe everyone, when they won't realise I am doing it.

Now I am in bed, and in theory Fran might tell on me because I'm supposed to have put my light out thirty-five minutes ago, but I don't expect she will. Mum and Dad are still up, talking in the kitchen, and Fran is trying to listen. She keeps going out of the bedroom for no good reason, like pretending she has forgotten to brush her teeth when I can already smell toothpaste on her breath. Then she hangs around in the hall, looking at the shelves out there and slowly, v-e-r-y slowly, choosing a book.

It never works, I'd tell her that if she asked me. Adults always know you're there, they have a sort of sixth sense, and they just don't talk about anything worth overhearing until you have gone away again. Like with Mum and Aggie, that time.

But there's an atmosphere all right. Something is going on, I'm sure of that. Fran can feel it too, that's why she's trying to listen.

Dad arrived with Aggie, then Don turned up and we all had dinner together. Mum cooked her chicken stew with mushrooms and little onions and garlic and wine, which I think might be Dad's favourite from when they were together, anyway it's mine too so I was happy. Don brought a bottle of red wine and Mum let me and Fran have a little bit of wine in our water like they do in France. To be completely honest I don't like wine but if it's just a splash in the water glass you can't taste it and it feels grown-up. You can't taste the wine in Mum's stew either, but she says adding it improves the main flavour, like garlic does.

Dad was impressed with our bedroom and I could see he was happy because *we* were happy, me and Fran that is. (In fact 'happy' is an overstatement but it *is* truer than it was.) He doesn't always bring us presents but this time he gave us personal CD players so we can listen to music at the same time in the same space and not bother each other. And he gave us classical music CDs, mine is recorders and Fran's is pianos, like our lessons. To inspire us, Dad said.

While we had dinner I forgot to watch out for clues, like I'd planned, because it was fun with everyone there. One thing *was* strange, though. When I reminded Mum about taping her interview there was a sort of awkward silence for a moment, and Mum and Dad looked down at their plates and Aggie and Don started up a new conversation out of nowhere – but after dinner Aggie and Don suddenly went, and I had the feeling they were leaving Mum and Dad together to talk, so that probably explains it. There was another silence when we'd had our ice cream, and the grown-ups looked at each other, and then Don sprang up and said, 'Aggie, we should go!' and whisked her into the hall. I heard them muttering at each other as they put their coats on and then Don called out, 'Thanks again, great meal, Emma!' to Mum and they were off out the door, so fast that Aggie left her big soft shawl thing behind. She'd had it over the back of her chair at dinner and it had fallen on the floor. So I picked it up and followed them outside to give it back to her.

Aggie and Don were arguing at the bottom of the front steps; I heard their voices as soon as I opened the outside door. I was embarrassed, and I wondered if they'd mind that I saw them fighting, and if I should just toss Aggie's shawl to her or run down and give it to her, or what. I am trying to explain that I didn't exactly *intend* to be a nosy parker and listen to them. But I did take advantage of the fact that it was dark, and that they were so busy quarrelling they didn't hear me come outside.

Don was saying, 'They're only trying to do what's best,' but Aggie interrupted him before he'd finished and she sounded crosser than I'd ever heard her.

'Well, *Emma* doesn't think it's best!' she sort of hissed at him. 'And *she's* the one who has to decide! We've agreed that!'

'Aggie, you know that's not true,' Don said, trying to pat her on the shoulder. She pulled away as though he'd bitten her and made a little snorty noise like she was so frustrated she couldn't bear it a moment longer. And as she jerked away from him she twisted round and saw me on the steps clutching her shawl, and if I hadn't been upset I might have laughed because she did look comical, like a toddler having a tantrum.

Then of course they both shut up, and sort of smoothed out their faces for me. Aggie gave Don an almost-friendly push, looking at me and trying to laugh it off, saying something to me about '*Brothers!*' (Like I'd know about that, I *don't* think.) And then she took the shawl and gave me a quick hug and they went off in Aggie's car, and I went back inside.

I may be right about Don and Mum after all. Here's what I think about what I heard – what I've put in my notebook.

They must be Mum and Dad.

And *doing what's best* could mean, making the Big Secret public – like, announcing who the Mystery Man is.

And Mum might not want that, because it's embarrassing.

(But Don said to Aggie *that's not true*, so maybe it's *Dad* who doesn't want it to be announced?)

With Aggie on Mum's side, of course.

And if Don is involved in all this, it could mean he actually *is* the Mystery Man!

I bet Don was trying to tell Aggie he wanted to make The Big Secret public. He was probably going to say it out loud and he might even have, if Aggie hadn't seen me! And I think Aggie was trying to stop him, and protect Mum from interference like friends do, and Don was trying to stop *her* from doing that.

So Aggie must know the secret – well, of course she does, I realise now that Mum wouldn't keep it from her.

I expect even Dad knows. He must feel really bad about it.

I wonder if Fran knows? Since it's all about her, I think she should.

And it's my family, so I should know, too.

Dad's here until tomorrow night. I'll see if I can find a way to talk to him some time tomorrow.

13

It was fun today. I, Josie Green, hereby admit that as a fact. Which is a surprise to me because I didn't expect it to be anything like fun.

We all went to Fran's football match together, me and Mum and Dad. I couldn't talk privately to Dad because there wasn't a chance, but I didn't mind. In fact it was just as well, because I realised this morning that there was no way I wanted to ask him anything straight out, especially now that Aggie and Don's argument has moved the clues around in my mind.

There is another reason. When I got up this morning, and Dad came for breakfast, and the four of us were just sitting around eating and talking – well, all my ideas seemed daft. Almost like I'd been making it up. As though the me who's been worrying and wondering, and taking notes, and detecting every minute I can, and going on about fathers and children – as if *that* Josie lived in a parallel universe and not in my world at all. So I just stopped thinking about it all for a while.

Another surprise was, I actually enjoyed Fran's match once we got to the football field. We stood on the sidelines together and shouted encouraging things, like I shouted, 'Go Fran, go!' every time she ran up the field or was anywhere near the ball. And Dad shouted instructions about not being offside, wherever that is, and Mum punched the air and shouted, 'Yesss!' whenever Fran's team looked like they were winning, which might have been embarrassing but wasn't.

And Fran's team did win and they are now through to the finals. And Fran scored a goal, which was extra specially good. You could see how pleased she was that she'd done well when Dad was there to see her, when she came off the field all hot and sweaty with mud on her shirt and her hair on end. And I don't want to play myself, but I can see Fran's good at soccer and I can even admire that in her.

Dad took us off to the shopping centre and paid for another CD each in the music shop, and this time we chose whatever we wanted, and then we had lunch in the café. I don't mind Fran so much when Dad's around, because to be brutally honest she isn't mean to me when he's there. And OK, she hasn't actually been mean to me since we changed the room around, but that's not long ago. It could still change back to how it was, I don't want to be gloomy but it could happen.

But she's a different person with Dad.

Which, I now see, so am I.

In fact, I almost liked her today.

This is much later, and I've tried to go to sleep but I can't. Fran is asleep on the other side of the screen. I know she is because I can hear little snores from her and no way would she do that if she wasn't really asleep. She hates being told that she snores, which she sometimes does, and she always claims she doesn't.

A terrible thing has happened. It has nothing to do with today, or how Fran has been. It has everything to do with me.

Well – anyway, I'll explain. Aggie came round in the afternoon and we played cards, and she gave me some sparkly scrunchies for my hair, which is getting straggly now it's longer. She didn't act like she was still cross with Don and in fact she didn't even mention what had happened the night before. To be honest I didn't care either way, because we were all having a good time. Also, I won at cards.

Then Dad left to catch his train to Nottingham and Mum and Aggie went to drive him to the station and to bring back fish and chips for supper. Fran got in the bath to soak away the aches from when she had fallen over in the football match.

I was tidying up my family history project, writing out the questions neatly to go with the tape, but I wanted to finish my display photos too, for the wall. I wrote about me as a baby to go with the cute photo I found, and I've put Mum and Aggie in, and me and Fran and Dad, and I wrote captions for everyone. (I couldn't say what I wanted in the captions though, like *Is She My Sister?* or *Who Is Her Father?* under the photos of Fran. Like I said before that's confidential family detecting, and even just the idea of someone with a blabber mouth, like Nikki, finding out what I'm thinking about is a truly sickening thought.)

But not being able to mention the most interesting things made what I've done seem a bit dull, and I thought that adding more people would help. I knew we had photos of Mum's parents in the boxes in the hall, so I decided to add Nan and Gramp to my project even though they're dead, because – and this might sound strange but it's true – I suddenly remembered them, and how patient Nan was when she looked after us. And you know how I remembered about Aggie's mum? And her little cakes? Well now I remembered Nan reading to us, and how she'd do different voices for the people in the books, and make up stories about my teddies, and lots of stuff like that. She was great.

So I decided to add facts about them, like when they were born, because it's so long ago it's surprising, although nowhere as impressive as Nikki's great-great-grandfather in China, but *that* reminded me of something else. Mum keeps important documents, like her passport and the mortgage things, in a box file in her bedroom. That's where stuff about Nan and Gramp – her mum and dad – would be, too. She showed me their birth certificates once before. And I didn't want to wait until Mum got back with the fish and chips.

I wouldn't have looked in the box file if I'd thought I shouldn't.

I didn't think it was private. I honestly didn't. You could say that I *should* have thought so, if you want to, but I still didn't.

Anyway I went into Mum's room and got the file out of her cupboard and opened it, and started looking through. And I saw an envelope that said 'birth certificates' on it in Mum's writing. And I thought they were the ones for Nan and Gramp, so I looked at them. But they weren't for Nan and Gramp. They were for me and Fran—

And so I looked at them.

And Fran, well, Fran doesn't have a different father at all.

Fran's father is the same as mine.

But her mother isn't.

14

I wish I'd never started this. Trying to find out what Mum and Aggie were talking about – I wish I'd never heard them talking, and I wish I'd never tried to work it all out.

Being a detective isn't fun at all.

I thought I wanted to know, but now that I do know, I wish I didn't. I wish that more than I have ever wished for anything. But wishing won't change it, to be brutally and completely honest. I do know that.

At first I just sat on Mum's bed feeling shivery, like I was coming down with flu. My brain seemed to pack up and I couldn't think properly. I'd have a thought, like, *I never will be able to look at her again!* and it just kept running through my head like a tape loop. Then I'd think, *I have to get everything put back in the box now* but I just kept sitting there and staring at the wall.

In the end it was my fear that Fran would find me with everything spread out in front of me that got me moving again. I didn't know if *she* knew; I still don't. But I was so shocked and I didn't want to have to deal with her feelings too. So I put all the papers back into the box file the way I'd found them, and put the file back in the cupboard. I got back into the kitchen while Fran was still in the bath and I was sitting at the table with all my family history stuff spread out when Mum and Aunt Aggie arrived with the fish and chips.

No one was surprised when I wasn't hungry and went to bed early, because it had been a busy weekend. No one even seemed to notice that I was quieter than usual, except me.

But I couldn't sleep all night. I lay in bed, and what I had discovered went round and round in my head on that non-stop tape loop. I thought about how much I didn't want to know what I *did* now know. I felt so anxious and sick that my stomach was sore with it. I probably slept a bit, Mum says that you always do even when you think you don't. But I stared at the ceiling a lot, and listened to Fran's snore-y breathing on the other side of the screen. And I couldn't avoid thinking about her any more.

I wondered, *does she know?* I wondered what she thought about it all, if she *did* know.

She must know, she simply *must*.

Which means it was only *me* who didn't.

I wondered if Fran knew that I hadn't had a clue about it, all these years. Then I tried to work out how I could possibly *not* have known – why no one had told me. How I hadn't guessed the real truth, even as a detective.

By the time morning came I felt as though the inside of my brain had been rubbed with sandpaper.

Even Mum, who usually doesn't notice stuff like that, unless you fall over or do something very obvious like walk into a wall, even she said I looked pale when I got up. I couldn't look her in the face to agree with her, though. She felt my forehead to see if I had a temperature, which I didn't, and then said maybe I was sickening for something and if I wasn't well at school I should go to the sickroom and get the nurse to call her.

I couldn't avoid Fran once we were up, although I felt nervous and embarrassed. Like I was wearing a big sign around my neck that said *I KNOW YOUR SECRET,* even though I wasn't. (Well, *doh!* of course I wasn't.) And even though there was no way Fran could guess what had happened.

But she does know something's wrong, she kept looking at me when we were having breakfast. She even tried to be nice to me because she thought I was sick. She actually poured me some juice instead of nicking it all for herself like normal, but I couldn't drink it.

I felt weird all day. I couldn't eat any lunch and I couldn't concentrate. People would say stuff to me and I would think I was listening to them, but then I'd realise I hadn't heard anything and they'd have to say it all again, or walk off in a huff like Nikki because she thought I was being rude.

At first Bryony kept on asking me what was wrong, but I didn't tell her and after a while she shut up. But then instead of nagging she was really kind, and carried my bag and stopped other people going on at me, and that all made me feel like crying. I wanted to tell her, because she was being such a good friend. But I didn't know where to start the story. So I just concentrated on not crying, because I thought if I started I'd never stop.

By the afternoon, though, I thought I might faint instead of cry. Not that I have ever fainted, but how I felt was probably like people who faint feel, just before their legs sag and they fall over unconscious. The room was shifting around at the sides of my eyes, sort of coming and going. I put my head down on my desk, and I heard Bryony tell Ms Macintosh, and then the nurse came and took me out of class and I lay down in the sickroom until the end of the day.

I went to sleep for a while, and I did feel a bit better when I woke up. The nurse took my temperature and asked me about aches and pains, and when I didn't have any of those she asked me did I have troubles at home. But I just shook my head; I couldn't tell her anything.

The nurse called Mum when I was in the sickroom. She phoned her again after I woke up feeling better; I could hear her chatting away in her office. Lots of 'Oh, I think so too, Mrs Green', and 'They often do, don't they?' and 'Best to be sure, Mrs Green'.

I can't imagine chatting away happily to Mum ever again in my life. Not about anything that matters.

How could it be true?

How could they not have told me?

The worst bit of how I feel – and it might sound strange, but it's true – is this.

It's like I have discovered that I'M the one who doesn't fit. That it's ME who isn't truly part of our family.

I know that Fran isn't my sister after all. (Well, she is really, it's silly to say she isn't, but it's not how I thought it was going to be.) But my family isn't how I thought it was either – not how I used to think it was, and not how I suspected it was, either.

Neither of those was true.

And that means that *everyone* but me knew, and nobody told me. Which is what makes me feel like it's *me* that doesn't belong.

I suppose I can't be completely certain that Fran knows her own secret but I think she does; I suppose that's why Aunt Aggie said Fran was jealous of me. It could be true, and this could be the reason: because I am Mum's daughter and she, Fran – she isn't.

I thought I'd feel better if I discovered the reason, but I don't. I feel worse, because of being left out of the truth. Like I wasn't worth telling. Like I wasn't important. And that feels really *really* terrible, and I don't know what to do about it.

I can't talk to Mum.

I don't want to talk to Aggie.

I can't talk to Fran.

And I can't even tell Bryony.

The only thing I can think of doing is to find Dad and talk to him about it. As it turns out, he's actually the one who must know everything! How weird is *that*.

Even if it's really hard to get the words out and ask the right questions, I *have* to try to talk to – well, someone, and it looks like it has to be Dad.

I can't keep this to myself, I think I'd burst.

I'll go to Nottingham and find Dad.

I'll make him tell me the truth. All of it.

15

When I was six I broke Mum's bathroom radio, and it wouldn't switch off any more no matter what you did. It was new, the radio, and I was upset about what I'd done so I pretended it hadn't been me. I said I hadn't touched it and it must have just broken on its own.

I felt sick about that for three days; I had a sort of lump in my throat like when I had tonsillitis, and another one in my stomach. When I finally told Mum that it had been me after all she was cross, but I didn't care because I was relieved I didn't have to keep the secret any more.

So I hope that when I talk to Dad I'll start to feel better. It will be hard to start off with, but right now is horrible anyway. Feeling sick because I know something isn't any fun at all. It's like a worm gnawing away inside me. If a worm had teeth to do any gnawing.

I wish I was on the other side of this, I wish I'd already done it – found Dad, said what I want to say, asked what I have to ask. I wish I was looking back afterwards. But I'm not afterwards, I'm now. I'm in bed reading back through all my notes and clues and theories. Trying to make sense of them. Trying to work out if I *should* have known.

Last night I thought I'd been wrong about everything, but today I can see that my ideas weren't completely wrong. In fact I got some things right, even if – to be honest – I didn't realise that at the time.

You know how sometimes you know things without putting them into words? You just sort of *feel* them. Or like, if you do try to put them into words you can get the feelings true, even if the words aren't exactly right.

For instance.
Fran knows that I know – *something*.
She just doesn't know *what* I know.

For another instance.
I did know there was something wrong with the idea that Fran was jealous of me. I just didn't know what was wrong, or what might be right instead.

And for that matter, I *did* know there was a family secret. And if anyone had bothered to tell me the truth, or even just given me a hint about it, I wouldn't have got that wrong either.

I haven't phoned Dad to tell him that I'm coming; if I did he would tell Mum, and I don't want her to know what I'm doing. First of all because she'd try to stop me, and second of all because I'd have to tell her why.

And third of all because I am so angry about being lied to that I want to hurt her, which running away, even just to see Dad, will do.

OK, I can admit that maybe I shouldn't have opened the envelope that said 'birth certificates' and looked inside it. But Mum should have told me the truth ages ago. So I still feel a tiny bit guilty about the envelope, but that's now been swamped by being angry with Mum. And everyone else.

You might think I should be angry with Dad as well as Mum. And I am, but it's a different kind of angry. I live with Mum, like, 24/7 – and she didn't tell me, every *day* she didn't tell me, although she had the chance. That feels worse than Dad not saying, because he's not around much to tell me anything anyway.

It shouldn't be a surprise to find out – what I have found out – about my own family.

I'm going this morning. I'll go to school first, but I'll walk out after assembly and go to the station. No one will think I'm absent because they will have seen me in assembly; they'll just think I'm in the toilets or back in the sickroom. I can get to St Pancras station with my travel pass and then get a train to Nottingham. They go all day.

I'll take a change of clothes in my school backpack. And a bottle of water and some crisps and sweets from home, because snacks are expensive when you buy them on the train. And, no surprise, I'll take my notebook with me. Not just because I need to keep it safe; I also want to write the end of the story in it.

When I've got the answers I need, I'll be able to write down the actual truth, about everyone.

I don't know how to face Fran. Or Aggie. Ever again.

It's just too weird.

Last night I wondered if I'd stay up in Nottingham for ever. To be brutally honest I don't suppose I *could* actually live with Dad. But this morning I realised I didn't want to anyway, because of being angry and upset with him as well.

In fact I am angry with my entire family.

What kind of family keeps one person from knowing a secret that the *whole* of the rest of *everyone* else must know? I could just spit at them all, every single one of them, even Don whose fault this is not, although I now realise that he knows as well; that's what he must have been on about with Aggie, in the street the other night.

The other night!

It seems years ago now.

So I got to school with my running-away plan ready in my head. I felt slightly guilty saying goodbye to Mum as usual, and walking to the bus stop with Fran as usual, but it was easier than I thought it would be. A bit of me wanted to say to Mum, *Look! I have clothes in my bag! I'm running away!* But of course I didn't. And a tiny part of me wanted Mum to guess what I was doing and stop me. I even imagined Fran turning to me at the bus stop and saying, *Don't go, Josie!* But of course she didn't either, and one of her friends was at the bus stop so they talked to each other and I could be quiet. Which I wanted.

Leaving after assembly wasn't that easy. I had forgotten it was PE, when our class stays in the hall instead of leaving with everyone else. But when the others were getting the mats out of the cupboard I just – walked out. And no one noticed, not even Bryony, because I waited until she was in the changing room. No one stopped me when I walked across to the gate, as bold as brass as Dad would say, and started off down the road.

Then I felt wonderful, like I had won a race! I felt free and excited and I almost forgot why I was running away. For a minute or two, anyway.

Getting to our station was OK but then I started to worry about the next step: St Pancras, and how I'd find the Nottingham platform, and stuff like that. I don't want to sound feeble but I'd never done it by myself and I didn't want to ask anyone too many questions in case they came back with, *And why are you not at school, young lady?* I thought there might be people looking out for school truants, and I was wearing my uniform so I stuck out. But I had twenty minutes to wait for the local train anyway so I decided to soothe my nerves with a chocolate muffin, however much it cost, from a stall out the front with tables and chairs. I broke the muffin up into tiny bits to make it last longer, and remembered being in the smart café in the shopping centre with Aggie, and how delicious their muffins were, much better than this one.

And then suddenly I saw her. Walking across from the car park into the station. She was dressed in the clothes she puts on when she needs to impress people – that's what she says, that she dresses for the old razzle dazzle. A black suit and a big swirly coat, and her shawl thing flung over her shoulders, and those wickedly wonderful high-heeled boots with tassels. She had her briefcase – the big one that she puts her laptop in – and a Starbucks cup in the other hand, and I thought she must be off on a trip for her job, striding along and looking like a million dollars, as she would most probably have said herself; I could almost hear her voice saying that in my head.

It's hard to believe because it was such a weird moment, but it really was Aggie. Although afterwards I realised – well, not *that* weird a moment. She lives near us, between us and the station, in fact. She parks her car and goes into work by train most days, and I knew that. Still, at the time it seemed very strange, and somehow like a sign. (Though I didn't know what it was a sign of, so it was more like what I said before – having feelings without knowing the words that matched them.)

And for a nanosecond I felt like I was split into two different people, and I didn't know which of them was me.

One part of me was the Josie who wanted to jump up and call out to her. It felt like something I couldn't *not* do, like a sort of instinct that you do without thinking.

The other part of me was the Josie who never wanted to talk to Aggie again. Not ever. Not in my whole life to come.

But I *didn't* think about it, I just did what the first rush of feelings told me.

I jumped up and called out to her.

'*Aggie!*'

Really loud, just like that.

And she heard me; I could see her sort of hesitate in her stride as my voice registered in her mind. Then she swung around and searched around with her eyes, trying to match what she'd heard with a face, and looking like she knew whose voice it was but not believing she could be right.

When she found me in the crowd her face sort of lifted, and she smiled and waved, and mimed surprise, like *What are you doing here?* Then she started to walk towards me looking pleased and I felt pleased for a moment myself, before I remembered that I was *not* pleased with her, that I was angry and hurt and confused. And then I was sorry I'd called out because now I'd have to confront her about everything, when part of me wanted to keep admiring her and having her as my honorary aunt.

Even though I knew in my heart I couldn't do that any more.

Even though I wanted to be the Great Detective, and prove I'd worked out everything.

I think I'll remember that moment for ever; how awful I felt.

'Josie! What are you doing here?'

There was a bit of a pause. I didn't answer right away because, to be absolutely honest, I didn't know what to say. I didn't know where to start explaining. The only thing I thought of saying was, *What are YOU doing here?* Which would have made me sound like an echo chamber. So I didn't say anything.

Aggie stared at me some more, and then she plonked her briefcase beside my little table and sat down opposite me. She uncapped her coffee cup and looked inside it, and she put it down again. She glanced up at me, and then looked away. I could see that she felt *something* was wrong between us, even though she didn't know what – she couldn't possibly have done. Then she cleared her throat, just like in one of those clunky

TV soaps when they are signalling that someone is going to say something important.

'Does Emma know where—'

'I'm running away,' I hissed at her, not wanting anyone else to hear me. 'So of *course* Mum doesn't know.'

'Oh,' said Aggie quietly. She picked up her coffee again and sipped it, and there was another awkward silence.

I knew I had to explain, and I didn't know where to begin, so I just said it in the simplest way I could.

'I found the birth certificates,' I said, looking her straight in the face. I watched her expression change as it sank in, what I meant. I even saw her jaw tighten for a moment, which was still like something on TV. Not like my real life.

'Whose birth certificates?' she asked, but I could tell that she knew.

'Mine,' I said. 'Mine – and Fran's!'

'You found *Fran's* birth certificate?'

I nodded. Aggie had a funny expression on her face, and it's hard to name it. Not exactly embarrassed, and not exactly horror-struck. Maybe a bit of both.

'So now I know,' I said. 'I know who you are. You're really Fran's mother, aren't you?'

16

It was at that exact moment I realised how angry I was with her.

Aggie had been my special grown-up friend, my very own chosen aunt, and the one grown-up person I could talk to. Or so I had thought. Well, not any more.

'Fran knows the truth, right?' I said.

Aggie nodded. 'She's known for ages. For ever, really. Well, ever since she was old enough to understand…'

Her voice trailed away and her eyes filled with tears. She put her hands up to her face and clutched her cheeks and sort of dabbed at her eyes. She smudged her eye make-up, I couldn't help noticing.

'I'm so sorry, Josie,' she whispered. 'We should have told you ages ago.'

If I hadn't been angry I would have been sorry for her. But I didn't feel sorry at all, because until then most of my angry hurt feelings had been about Mum. Now I realised that I felt even worse about Aggie, and it all flooded out.

'How could you and Mum *not* tell me?' I asked with my voice rising, although I'd meant to keep it down.

Aggie's tears were dripping down her cheeks. Her mascara was running but I didn't tell her. I didn't feel like helping.

'Fran was— Fran was only little,' Aggie said. 'And Emma thought – well I did too – we thought you needn't be told until later on.' She shifted in her seat, and kind of squared her shoulders, and corrected herself. 'No. That's not true. The truth is, Josie, it was *me*, not Emma. I didn't want anyone to know who didn't already – didn't have to know, I mean.'

She glanced at me, and added, 'When you were both little it didn't seem to matter. And it stayed that way. Because of me, really. We were discussing it again the other night, your mum and dad and me. Trying to decide what to do. We were worried about your family research; that you might find out something that way. I am truly sorry, Josie,' she said again. 'I know it must have been a shock.'

'A SHOCK?' I had jumped to my feet by then,

128

and I was just about yelling at her. 'A *shock* to find out that my sister isn't *really* my true sister? That you are actually Fran's *mother*?'

I jabbed my finger right in Aggie's face; I was so carried away. She flinched, but she didn't pull away.

'You said Fran was *jealous* of me, and I thought that was because of *me*, that I'd done something wrong. And all the time, *all the time*, there was this enormous – this great lumping *elephant of truth* sitting there and you couldn't be honest with me about it. You and Mum both, you've treated me like I was a stupid baby. As though I didn't count!' I could feel tears welling up but I was determined not to cry before I had finished. 'You lied to me! You left Fran! You left *your own baby*! How could you?'

People had started to stare, but to be brutally honest I didn't care. Aggie reached across the table to grab my hand, but I shook her off.

'And what about you and Dad? He was married to Mum, and you had his baby! I thought Mum was your *best friend*!'

Aggie jumped up then and leaned forward over the table, like she was going to say something, but I just rolled my own words over the top of her.

'Oh no! Don't explain it to me *now*!' I shouted. 'Not now you *have* to, now I've found you out!

You wouldn't tell me, so now I'm going to see Dad. And don't try to stop me, because I won't let you!'

But as I was shouting those words I realised that I didn't want to go and talk to Dad at all. Because, what did he know? About my real life? He was part of the whole mess, I could see that, but I couldn't see how he'd help me sort it out.

But I couldn't stay a moment longer with Aggie. You know how people say, *they were beside themselves*? That's how I felt. I could sort of see how I was yelling and stamping my foot at Aggie and being immature and ridiculous, but I didn't care.

'Actually, I've changed my mind! I'm not going to Nottingham after all!' I shouted. '*You* go, why don't you? You're all in this together, all you so-called grown-ups, and I hate you all! I don't want to talk to any of you!'

And then I turned and ran out of the station. I didn't know where I was going, I only knew I had to get away.

17

The truth was, I didn't know what to do next. I had run away from school, and now I was running away from Aggie *and* from the station before I'd even got on a train – to say nothing of running away from Dad, too, and I'd been running *towards* him until just a few minutes before!

But I felt a whole lot better than I had. Shouting at Aggie had got rid of a big wodge of anger from my soul, which funnily enough is what Aggie might have said if *she* had done the shouting. I've never been much of a shouter before, but I think I might take it up.

I stopped to think. I wasn't going to Nottingham any more, and I didn't want to go back to school and pretend nothing had happened.

Then I realised two things at the same moment. The first one was that I couldn't stand in the street for ever, but while I was still standing there, the second idea slid into the side of my mind.

I wanted to talk to Fran.

I know that might sound crazy. After all, talking to Fran hasn't exactly been my speciality, has it? But once I'd thought the thought, it took hold. More than anything, I wanted to talk to someone who understood how I felt.

And I suddenly knew that person – the only one – was Fran.

So I thought I'd go back to school after all, which looking back now I can't help but think, *Wow! That was a sadly boring idea!* but it seemed right at the time. I even planned to sneak back in and find Fran and make her talk to me, which shows how desperate I was.

But I'd just started walking back up the road towards the shopping centre to catch the bus to school when I heard the *vroom!* of Aggie's car in the road behind me. I just kept walking. I even thought that if I crossed over the main road and took a side street, I'd get away from her in the one-way system—

'Josie! *Please!*'

Aggie was driving her car along really slowly beside me, trying to keep pace with me. When I didn't answer or stop walking she pulled over and parked, and then ran after me. A bit like a cop show on TV, I couldn't help thinking.

I started to walk really quickly, but even with those heels on she still caught up. She grabbed my arm and swung me round so fast I almost banged into her. Her face was streaming with tears; I admit I was shocked at how she looked.

'I won't try to stop you,' Aggie sobbed at me. I almost laughed, it was such a silly thing to say – she HAD stopped me.

'You're wrong about one thing,' she went on, 'and I have to tell you! Me and your Dad, that was *before* he got together with Emma. They...I was sick, for ages after I had Fran. In and out of the hospital, on pills, everything. And Emma and David took over, they looked after her when she was a tiny baby, and—' She sort of gulped, and dashed her hand over her face, smearing more of her make-up; she looked like a wild woman.

'I'd *never* have taken David away from Emma; you have to know. Please believe me, Josie!'

Even then my very first thought wasn't, *Poor Aggie*, although it could have been because she was in such a state. My first thought was, *What about Fran? Never mind what I think about what you did or didn't do – what about your daughter Fran?* (OK, I do admit that the next thought tumbling into my head was, *What about ME and the lies you've told me?*)

I couldn't help feeling slightly sorry for this tear-smeared and miserable Aggie. But it was like I was still those two different people I'd been, back at the railway station. One of them *was* sorry for Aggie, but the new Josie Green, the one in charge, was too angry and hurt to care about her. I pulled myself away from Aggie's clutching hand.

'You left her!' I shouted. 'Your own baby!'

'I was sick!' Aggie shouted back. 'Please listen to me – let me explain.'

'You lied to me!' I shouted again. 'You're such a cow! I don't want to hear any more of your lies!'

I was crying so hard by then, and I couldn't bear to stay with her a moment longer. I turned and ran up the road, and this time Aggie didn't follow me. I expected the *vroom!* of her car again behind me, and when it didn't come I thought she'd given up, although I should have remembered what Mum says about Aggie's single-mindedness. She hadn't given up – she'd called in more troops instead, because when I got up to the main road there was Mum's car at the corner. She saw me and drove down to meet me. Which seemed even more like a movie – you know, 'Target sighted! Woman down!' That sort of thing.

I felt sort of doomed, and I knew Mum would start in on me in a serious way. I suppose I could have tried running off again but she jumped out of her car and ran towards me, clutching her mobile to her ear and yammering something into it. I braced myself for, *And what do you think you've been doing, my girl?* So I was amazed when she flung her arms around me and hugged me instead.

'Josie!' she sobbed. 'I thought – when Aggie called me – oh darling, you're safe and I've found you.' Then she pulled back a bit, and looked me straight in the eye.

'Don't say anything yet,' she went on. 'I don't blame you for running away, and I'm sorry, I am *so* sorry. We should have told you. You're right to be upset and I expect you're angry with me as well as Aggie – with everyone. But I'm going to sort this out once and for all, and when I've had a chance to explain, I'll ask you to forgive me.'

Well, I still wanted to find Fran, more than I wanted to talk to Mum, to be brutally honest. But I thought I'd hear Mum out first, and see if I could get it all straightened out in my mind. There was still some detecting to do, after all.

Have you ever been to one of those outdoor plays that moves around – with the actors going from place to place and the audience following along? I went to one in Nottingham once, with Dad. It started off in the street and moved around the town. One scene was out in a field, and one was inside a house, and in the end we all walked behind the actors carrying candles and singing. And the reason I ask, is because that's more or less how the day went on after that – minus the candles and singing. It wasn't fun though; it was just exhausting.

I've never argued or listened or cried so much in my whole life. By the end of the day we were all just about wrung out to dry, which is how Dad put it, and I agree. It's funny how I once worried that the true story of my life might be boring. I have to admit this part of it has been the complete opposite.

Mum whisked me off to the posh café in the shopping centre, and then Aggie turned up too.

I did *not* want her there; I said we needed Fran, not Aggie. But Mum said that if Aggie *was* there they'd both answer my questions, and then we'd get Fran out of school and talk again. So I agreed. The wait persons in the café must have regretted having us though. We sat for so long, talking and crying and then starting all over again, which must have put off the other customers. They did bring us little cakes we hadn't ordered to cheer us up, and one of them kept patting me on the shoulder when she passed. But I plan never to go to that café again, or at least to wait for years into the future until I have changed so much I am unrecognisable to them.

Anyway, I got stuck straight into detecting because I wanted to finish it all off in my notebook later on. Was it really true what Aggie had said in the street, that she'd been with Dad before Mum?

And Mum said it *was* true. They – Dad and Aggie – were living together and everything, way before they had me. 'And way before your dad and I were an item,' she added, 'but of course we did know each other.' I certainly believed that – I'm willing to bet no one's ever known Aggie without getting to meet Mum as well. But I'd never have guessed about Aggie and Dad in a squillion years. It was hard to imagine, but the more Mum talked – with Aggie nodding and sobbing and blowing her nose – the more I could sort of see them together. And the way they are now with each other – kind of up and down? Spiky one day and friendly the next, instead of the same all the time? That could be a clue too – well, *now* it could be a clue; it wasn't one before.

Some detective I've been, I *don't* think.

'But then you had a baby, right?' I asked, turning to Aggie. She nodded.

'With Dad?'

She nodded again.

'And then – what?' I asked. 'You just – *left your baby*?' I didn't bother to hide what I thought about that.

Aggie did try to answer me. The trouble was, she couldn't get the words out. She kept gritting her teeth and then stopping to blow her nose and do some deep breathing to try to calm herself down. I'd never seen this side of her, not caring about her hair sticking up and her make-up wrecked, and to be brutally honest it freaked me out. But Mum took over, which I appreciated, although I didn't let her know that.

Mum patted Aggie's hand and said, 'Shall I do this bit?' And Aggie just nodded but I could tell she was so relieved she almost started sobbing again.

Anyway, what Mum explained was, right after she'd had Fran, Aggie got sick, like she'd told me. Mum said that it's something that can happen after women have babies, it's an illness with a name called postnatal depression, which is Latin, and means *after giving birth*. It's all down in my notebook now, of course.

Mum said it just happens out of the blue, and what it means is, the women who get it are so depressed they can't look after themselves, let alone their babies. And while Mum patted Aggie's hand some more and made soothing noises, I saw something I hadn't ever noticed before. Mum was treating Aggie like she'd treat me or Fran if we were sick. She looks after Aggie like she's *her* mother!

Well, they both look after each other in a way, that's what friends do. But without Mum, Aggie – well, I suddenly saw that without Mum, Aggie couldn't cope. All her Fashion Queen clothes and her touchy feely talk, and her high-powered job – it's a sort of shell for the frightened person who is Aggie underneath. And now that I have experienced for myself being two different people at once, I can see how it could be true for Aggie as well.

Anyway, watching Mum calm Aggie down did impress me. And when I said *again* how I thought Fran should be there, this time Mum agreed. Even though Aggie was still in a state and Mum didn't want to leave her alone.

Mum said we'd go and get Fran so we could finish explaining with her there too, and that Dad was on his way down too, because she'd phoned and asked him to come.

'This is a family thing,' Mum said firmly. 'It's a bit late to say so, I know, but we have to deal with it as a family. All of us.'

18

I felt awkward while Mum was driving me and Fran home. I was nervous about how Fran would be with me, and she hadn't even looked my way since she got in the car. I didn't know how much Mum had explained when she'd picked her up from school.

Then Mum said, 'I'll phone Dad when we get home and see when he'll be here.'

And Fran said, 'I didn't know he was coming!' She sounded pleased.

And I said, 'He wouldn't have had to if I'd gone up to see him, like I planned.' It was a sort of joke.

There was silence for a moment. Then Fran turned around from the front seat and looked me straight in the eye.

'You were going up to see Dad?'

I nodded.

'Why? To get him on *your side?*'

She looked completely furious. I just gaped at her. For once, I was speechless.

'You selfish little *cow*!' said Fran. 'I *hate* you for that!' And she turned back to the front and wouldn't look at me, or say another word.

Mum tried her soothing routine, but it didn't work this time. She wouldn't take it back, or explain what she'd meant.

I'd thought Fran was the one who'd understand, but now I wasn't so sure. This was not a good omen for the cosy family chat that was supposed to come next.

Fran leapt out of the car as soon as Mum found a parking spot, and ran inside. I went after her but she just rushed into our room and slammed the door in my face. And then Aggie arrived as well, and I started to feel frantic because I thought it was hopeless; I'd never get a chance to talk to Fran.

But Mum sorted it out. (She really is a superstar soother. If she got a job soothing countries down we probably wouldn't have wars.) She made Aggie lie down on her bed for a rest, and she got Fran out of the bedroom and sitting at the kitchen table. Fran wouldn't say anything at first, and she still looked furious, but at least she was there.

And we went on with the story.

Mum started with when she and Dad got together, when Aggie was in the hospital and they were looking after baby Fran between them. Then she looked at us both, and gave a big sigh.

'You know, I'm not trying to make excuses,' said Mum. 'This secret has been kept far too long, and it should never have been one in the first place. But we were worried about hurting Aggie, and when she was better and left hospital for good, it was still hard to tell her the truth. But then we found – well—'

Fran had been quiet, but then she jumped up so fast that her mug of tea rocked right off the table. She was almost spitting, she was so upset.

'Oh, *right!*' she shouted, pink in the face with fury. 'Let's have the *truth!* I know this bit off by heart! How Aggie didn't mind AT ALL about you and Dad, and she wasn't BOTHERED about being with Dad any more, and she was perfectly FINE with giving up her baby. Her baby was ME! How can you just talk about it like I was a *parcel!*'

Mum was on her feet too by then, and she grabbed Fran and held her tight.

'*That's not fair!*' she shouted back. 'No one thought you were a parcel! Aggie *loved* you!'

143

Fran pulled away, but Mum went on at top volume.

'Aggie loved you!' she repeated. 'I *know* she did! As much as *I* love you! But she hadn't spent enough time with you when you were tiny, and she hadn't had the bonding time mums need with babies. And in her heart, she didn't trust herself to be a good mother, after what had happened.'

She grabbed Fran again and hugged her, and Fran didn't pull away this time. I could see why she'd find this bit of the story so upsetting. Well you would, wouldn't you? If you were the baby that got given up?

'So you stayed with me and David a while longer,' Mum said to her softly. 'And the 'while longer' turned into a year. And when Aggie finally got a job again she had to travel a lot – like the one she's got now – so she *couldn't* have you with her. And when I got pregnant with *you*, Josie,' Mum added, turning to me but still holding on to Fran, 'it was lovely that we could still have Fran. David and I knew we wanted the both of you. So Aggie gave Fran up officially and David and I got legal custody, and we got married as well. Fran was ours by then anyway, as far as we felt. As much as you were, Josie, when you arrived.'

Mum took a big breath.

'I love you both, Fran *and* you, Josie. You are both my beloved daughters. You always will be.' Her voice had gone wobbly, but she went on anyway.

'I know it's been a shock, Josie, finding out the way you did. And hard for Fran, all these years. I wanted to tell you, but I'd promised Aggie and she was terrified of people knowing. She *knew* she had to let the truth out some time, but she kept putting it off, and putting it off... She does try her best, you know.'

There was a small silence. Then Fran pulled away from Mum, and looked straight at me.

'Oh *right*,' she said, sort of hissing. 'Just like *Little Miss Perfect* here, I suppose, always trying to do what's best! *Best for her*, that is. I hate you both!' And she stormed out of the room.

Now I understand more about how Fran felt. I can see that *of course* Fran didn't like everything finally coming out. I wouldn't like it myself if I'd been sitting a geography test and someone dragged me out of school because my Big Secret was out. And specially if it was my smarty-pants younger sister who had turned into an ace detective and Discovered Everything.

But at the time I was still trying to take everything

in. I knew I wanted to talk to Fran – I still wanted to – but that was for my sake, not hers. Even the fact that Fran's whole past had been a secret most of her life – and maybe she'd *liked* it like that – hadn't really sunk in.

And Fran being Fran, she was used to *not* saying how she felt unless she was absolutely driven to it. I use lots more words than Fran; I know that. It's not better or worse; we're just different. And to be brutally honest, I wanted to talk to her because I thought she'd understand *me*, I didn't see that I needed to understand *her* too.

I followed Fran into our bedroom. I minded what she'd said but I thought I understood why she was being so mean. She'd been carrying a secret that no one would choose to have, if they could choose. And maybe she truly *was* jealous of me, and I could finally see why she might be. And she'd had to cope with everything all by herself, for ages.

All that whizzed through my head at supersonic speed, the way thoughts can. But I didn't want to be Miss Perfect, not even to make Fran feel better, and I wanted to get a few more things straight as well.

'That's not true,' I said to the back of her head. She was staring out the window and didn't answer.

'It's not fair either,' I added. 'I *don't* just do

146

what's best for me, no more than *you* just do what's best for you. I don't even know what you meant about Dad, what you said in the car. On my side about *what*? I just wanted someone to tell me the truth!'

Fran made a sort of *humph!* noise at the window, and muttered something like, *it's all very well for you.* But I wasn't having that.

'Fran, can't you see? We've *both* been lied to, we've both been treated badly. This isn't like a competition – it's been hard on you, but it's been hard for me too, suddenly discovering something that everyone else has known for ever.'

'Not everyone,' said Fran to the window.

'OK, not everyone,' I agreed. 'But everyone who matters in this family, except for me. How do you think *that* felt?'

'Yeah – but Dad – when you said about going to talk to him—'

'So?' I asked. 'I don't get it.'

Fran glanced over her shoulder at me. Then she shrugged, and turned around and looked at me.

'Dad's special.'

I still didn't get it. She could see that, but for once she didn't get impatient or snippy with me.

'Dad's special to me,' Fran said, looking serious. 'He – Dad – I was *always* his,' she added. 'I was

Aggie's, and I still am for that matter. But not really, not how it counts. And I'm Mum's too. I've always known that, but not – not like you are, whatever she says. But with Dad, it's different. I was always Dad's. Either way.'

'But Fran, don't you see? Dad's my father too, so whatever you think about the others, we actually *are* sisters! I thought I'd find out that we weren't, but now I see that we absolutely are. It has to count for something!'

Fran thought for a moment. Then she nodded, and gave me the ghost of a smile.

I wanted to ask her a million questions.

Like, *Did you always know?*

And, *How do you feel about Aggie now?*

And, *Is this why you wanted somewhere that was just your own, like Rose's flat?*

But I thought she might tell me anyway once we got along better, which I was now completely determined that we would.

'When did you guess, about me?' asked Fran, breaking the silence.

I told her the truth. 'I *didn't* guess. Well, I did, but I guessed the wrong things.'

'Like what?'

'Like, um, like Don was your father.'

Fran stared at me in disbelief. Then she raised

one eyebrow, just like Mum does. (I admit I felt a rush of envy – when had she managed to get that working?)

'Your hair's the same,' I said defensively, but I couldn't help laughing.

'Don has *fairy hair*?' snorted Fran, and then we were both laughing – me because Fran remembered what I used to call her hair when I was little, and Fran – well, I suppose she wanted to have something to laugh about, and Don as a fairy was a good place to start. (You wouldn't know, but Don is hunky and proud of his chest muscles, and not a good candidate for fairydom. And what I didn't think about until later was, Don is Fran's uncle, isn't he? So their hair *could* be the same, after all.)

'Josie, I don't really hate you. And, um, I'm sorry I called you a cow.'

'Well I called Aggie a cow today,' I offered.

'Not in front of Mum, I bet!'

There was another silence, a more comfortable one.

'Sometimes I've thought...' Fran didn't finish, so I nudged her shoulder.

'What? What did you sometimes think?'

'That you *should* know the real story. I even thought maybe I should tell you,' said Fran.

149

I stared at her in disbelief.

'*You* should have told me? No *way*, Fran! *They* should have told me, Mum and Dad. And Aggie. None of this is your fault, you know. It wasn't your job to put it right!'

'That's why you were so miserable the other night, isn't it?' Fran asked. 'You'd found out, hadn't you?'

I nodded. 'I still am miserable about it,' I told her. 'Like I wasn't a proper part of the family. But then…'

Fran finished my sentence.

'But then – yeah. So did I. That's how I felt.'

We sat on her bed and glanced at each other. Then Fran stuck her hand out. I took her hand and shook it, and then turned it into a high five.

'Pact,' I offered. 'Only the truth for us, from now on.'

'Because we're sisters, right?' she said.

'So we have to stick together,' I agreed. There was another silence.

'No pressure or anything, though,' I added, nudging her again.

And Fran grinned at me. A real smile.

19

Since then I have thought a lot about what happened, about trying to be a Family Detective and everything. I feel as though I've waited for years to work it all out. It isn't years though, it's actually only weeks, it just seems a lot longer. My hair hasn't even grown much while I've been thinking, which is a sorry disappointment.

Anyway, this finally is what I think is true.

The end of the mystery.

The truth about Josie Green.

Number One.

First of all, you might think you know someone really well and then you discover something new about them, something really big that you didn't know before. And you think *they* have changed, because you know this new thing. But they haven't changed at all. It's *you* that's changed.

That's like me with Aggie. Finding out about

her, what had happened to her and what she'd done – it turned my world on its head, and I didn't like that. But it really just meant I knew more about her, not that she had changed. She's been that person for ages; only I didn't know.

<u>Number Two.</u>
Second of all, I thought I hated Aggie when I first found out, but I don't any more. She had a horrible time being so sick, and she couldn't help that. And there are things that haven't changed, like how much I still admire how she looks, and how she does her job, stuff like that.

I don't trust her like I used to, and I don't suppose I ever will. But maybe the way I used to feel about her wasn't real. Maybe that whole thing I invented – Aunt Aggie, my honorary aunt, all that? Maybe it was just a game – like a story I was telling myself. Not real life. I think we both enjoyed it; Aggie liked having me looking up to her and I enjoyed doing the looking up. But like Bryony says about her life these days, it has Moved On since then. My life has, I mean. Well, so has Aggie's, for that matter.

At first, seeing Aggie was embarrassing. I kept thinking about all the shouting and crying, and how rude I'd been. (It's funny; I liked doing all that at the time, but I can see it's hard to know what to do after it's over.) I couldn't think how the new Josie Green would get along with the new Aggie.

It's got easier, though. The last time she was here I felt more ordinary with her. We even spent ages talking about my hair, which is the sort of conversation at which she excels. I want her to spend more time with Fran, which seems only fair. But when I told Bryony everything, which I did eventually, she said it wasn't any use trying to push Aggie and Fran back together, like she'd done with her parents. 'They have to work it out themselves,' she said. I expect she's right. She's got her kitten *and* her dad's come back, so she's definitely worth listening to.

Number Three.

Third of all is Mum. I don't feel the same about Mum either, but not in a bad way. The Mum I see now – it's like I can accept that she's other people *as well as* my Mum. Not that I want her to be, to be brutally honest, but she is. She'd do anything for Aggie, and I might not like that but I'm not going to say she shouldn't. It's how it's always been for her. And I know more about her than I did, and luckily it's all good. Like the soothing for Britain stuff. And how, in a crisis, Mum's the best person you could ever have on your side. You can see that if you think about what happened to baby Fran. What if Mum hadn't been there?

Number Four.
Fourth is Dad, and it's funny, but I mind about him the least. And why that's funny is, since he's the birth father for me and Fran, he should probably matter the most.

You might even say, well, it's all HIS fault! Taking up with Aggie and then with Mum, and having Fran and then me, and then going off and leaving everyone to sort of get on with it without him. But I've more or less gone off trying to blame any one person. It's more complicated than just one person.

We talked, Dad and me, when he got down from Nottingham that night. He was sorry about not telling me the truth, he honestly was. And he wanted to talk about it then and there, but by the time he arrived I'd had enough of truth and honesty. If you aren't used to all that crying and shouting it tires you out, and I was wrung out to dry, like he said. So I didn't say as much as I'd planned.

One thing *he* said, though, that I liked. He said he was proud of me. I didn't know what he meant; I thought he must know about the orchestra, which is more than I did at that stage (and I did get in, hurrah!) but it wasn't that. He said he had to admire my persistence, how I'd stuck to my guns and tried to work it out for myself. Mind you, he doesn't know everything I thought – like about him – and I'm not going to tell him, either.

And <u>Number Five</u> is Fran, though in another way, she's also Number One.

Fran and me? Well, Fran is still my sister, like Mum is still my mum and Dad is still my dad. And to be completely honest about her, I actually feel she's *more* of a sister than she ever was before, although technically I suppose you could say that she's less than she was. But I don't think of her as my half-sister. She's just my sister and that's it. Full stop.

We're not the same kind of people, and I don't expect we ever will be. So we will never be like best friends. She still snaps at me from time to time, particularly at breakfast, so for all I know she's not a morning person any more than I am. But I don't take the snapping so personally these days; I try not to anyway. And I have to say that knowing what's true helped us both in the end.

I am making an effort to be more interested in sports, and she has asked me what to read for her English reports at school. So we're both trying to put our best feet forward. Instead of stepping on each other's toes all the time.

When I read back through my notebook I can't believe I got so many clues so wrong, although I expect even professional detectives make lots of mistakes. What I mind most is where there were real clues staring me in the face, just begging to be noticed, only I wasn't looking at them. Or I was, but I had them upside down.

Like, OK, if I list them all I'd feel a complete failure, so I'll only mention one example, which is Fran and Don's hair, and I know I have banged on about that a lot, but just hear me out.

I could have put two and two together in a different way. If I had, I'd have got there.

Fran's hair.

Don's hair.

The photo with Don and Aggie, and their mum and dad, and Fran and me.

Don's mum's hair, now I've looked again, was the *exact* same fly-away floaty stuff. Fairy hair obviously runs in the family, but equally obviously (obvious *now*) Aggie didn't inherit it.

And of course, Don's mum equals Aggie's mum, equals Fran's granny.

Maybe clues are always like that, though? Look at them one way, they add up to an answer. Look at them another way, though, and hey presto! It's a different story.

Anyway, just because I got it wrong on paper doesn't mean I got it completely wrong. In another way, in what I felt, I got it right.

Ms Macintosh once said that truth is stranger than fiction. She meant that as a good thing, she was talking about what you read in books – things that don't sound likely, although real life is often much more amazing.

Now I know for sure that truth can be stranger than any story you'd write down. I couldn't have thought up the real secret in my life in a squillion years, and it was right under my nose.

If someone had told me this story before I knew it was mine, I'd have thought everyone in it was bonkers. Including me. Now I see that sometimes in life, things just happen, and people do the best they can with them. They might make things worse, even when they're trying to do the very opposite. You just have to try your best and persist, like Dad said.

I still plan to be a famous detective, or a famous historian.

Or even a famous musician, since I was chosen for the orchestra.

Anything's possible. I can see that now.

Orchard Red Apples

Utterly Me, Clarice Bean	Lauren Child	1 84362 304 8
Clarice Bean Spells Trouble	Lauren Child	1 84362 858 9
The Truth Cookie	Fiona Dunbar	1 84362 549 0
Cupid Cakes	Fiona Dunbar	1 84362 688 8
Chocolate Wishes	Fiona Dunbar	1 84362 689 6
My Scary Fairy Godmother	Rose Impey	1 84362 683 7
Shooting Star	Rose Impey	1 84362 560 1
You're Amazing Mr Jupiter	Sue Limb	1 84362 614 4
Do Not Read This Book	Pat Moon	1 84121 435 3
Do Not Read Any Further	Pat Moon	1 84121 456 6
Tower Block Pony	Alison Prince	1 84362 648 9
What Howls at the Moon in Frilly Knickers?	Emily Smith	1 84121 808 1
When Mum Threw Out the Telly	Emily Smith	1 84121 810 3

All priced at £4.99

Orchard Red Apples are available from all good bookshops, or can be ordered direct
from the publisher: Orchard Books, PO BOX 29, Douglas IM99 1BQ
Credit card orders please telephone 01624 836000
or fax 01624 837033 or visit our Internet site: www.wattspub.co.uk
or e-mail: bookshop@enterprise.net for details.

To order please quote title, author and ISBN
and your full name and address.
Cheques and postal orders should be made payable to 'Bookpost plc.'
Postage and packing is FREE within the UK
(overseas customers should add £1.00 per book).

Prices and availability are subject to change.